Hot (

A Rainey Daye Cozy Mystery, book 6

by

Kathleen Suzette

Books by Kathleen Suzette:

A Rainey Daye Cozy Mystery Series

A Pumpkin Hollow Mystery Series

Candy Coated Murder
A Pumpkin Hollow Mystery, book 1
Murderously Sweet
A Pumpkin Hollow Mystery, book 2
Chocolate Covered Murder
A Pumpkin Hollow Mystery, book 3
Death and Sweets
A Pumpkin Hollow Mystery, book 4
Sugared Demise
A Pumpkin Hollow Mystery, book 5
Confectionately Dead
A Pumpkin Hollow Mystery, book 6
Hard Candy and a Killer
A Pumpkin Hollow Mystery, book 7
Candy Kisses and a Killer
A Pumpkin Hollow Mystery, book 8
Terminal Taffy
A Pumpkin Hollow Mystery, book 9
Fudgy Fatality
A Pumpkin Hollow Mystery, book 10
Truffled Murder
A Pumpkin Hollow Mystery, book 11
Caramel Murder
A Pumpkin Hollow Mystery, book 12
Peppermint Fudge Killer
A Pumpkin Hollow Mystery, book 13
Chocolate Heart Killer
A Pumpkin Hollow Mystery, book 14

Table of Contents

Chapter One

"MY CIDER PUNCH IS GOING to knock 'em dead tonight," I said to Cade as I poured the cranberry juice into the crockpot.

Cade leaned over my shoulder, watching what I was doing. "Cranberry juice? I thought you said you were making hot apple cider?"

"I am. Actually, I'm making hot cider punch. It's got pineapple juice, cranberry juice, apple juice, and an assortment of spices, including whole cinnamon sticks to make it nice and spicy. You wait and see. It's a tasty treat."

"Is it going to be an adult beverage?" he asked, sounding hopeful.

I laughed. "No. I'm making a child-friendly version for the party. You can add what you want later."

Maggie, my Bluetick Coonhound, sat near my feet, looking up at me hopefully as I added ingredients to the crockpot. I reached a hand out and scratched her head.

Tonight was the annual fall party at the Sparrow Mountain Lodge. The lodge was owned by a local family and had two dozen cabins in the woods near the Snake River that could be rented by the night or week. The lodge itself had a large dining room, a recreation hall, and rooms that could be rented for parties or receptions. The fall party was held every October, and the price of admission was a dish to share with everyone and twenty dollars. The owners of the lodge provided the main dish, usually a roasted pig or other meat, and the money donated went to a local homeless shelter. I looked forward to it every year, and it would be more fun this year with someone to bring with me to snuggle with. Cade and I hadn't been dating long, but we were serious.

"So, what all are we going to do at this party? Is it adults only?" he asked, leaning on the kitchen counter. His chocolate-brown hair was neatly parted on the side, and he wore jeans and a red T-shirt.

"It's more of a family kind of get-together. There's a great big bonfire where we'll roast marshmallows, eat an assortment of yummy food, and all hang out and ooh and ah over the beautiful weather."

"Sounds like fun," he said. "Why aren't you making anything else?" He glanced around the kitchen.

"I made pumpkin bread and cranberry bread. I've been waiting all year to make these yummy fall treats," I said as I sprinkled some whole cloves into the punch. "You know me—I couldn't just make one dish."

"But it's not a Halloween party? I don't need a costume?" he asked.

I looked at him and grinned. "Did you want to wear a costume? Is that disappointment I hear in your voice?"

He chuckled. "No. Not even a tiny bit of disappointment. I was afraid I'd have to dress up as a mummy or Dracula."

"Never fear. The community center has a costume party on October 29th. Of course, the majority of the partygoers will be under twelve, but don't let that stop you from dressing up like a mummy and attending. You'll fit right in."

He chuckled. "I'll skip it. So when are we going to work on these floors?" he asked, looking at the chipped linoleum flooring in the kitchen. I had recently moved into a cute little cottage that still had a lot of original vintage touches. I wanted to update some of them, but keep the majority as is. The kitchen had cute scalloped-cut cupboards that had been popular in the forties. Of course, I was in love with the kitchen.

"I was thinking about that. I'm wondering if I can find some vintage reproduction linoleum online. If not, I think I'll try some tile. The linoleum in here has got to go. The chips and tears are too much to deal with. Oh, and I'm going to try to find some vintage wallpaper too."

"Wallpaper?"

"Yup. I want to make this kitchen look as authentic as possible, and without wallpaper, it won't look complete."

"The hardwood floors in the living room will have to be sanded and stained," he said, walking to the kitchen doorway and looking at the living room floor. "I think we can rent a floor sander down at the hardware store."

"That's a lot of work," I said, putting the lid back on the crockpot. I went to stand beside him.

"It is. But it's expensive to have a professional do the work," he said. "Besides, I'm handy. Kind of."

"I bet you can do anything you put your mind to. I love that you're handy with tools," I said, putting my arm around his waist. "I don't know what I'd do if I had to do it all on my own."

"I don't mind doing the work," he said and kissed me. Then he pulled back and looked at me.

"That's a serious look. What's up?" I asked.

"That ex-husband of yours. Is he gone?"

I eyed him. "He's gone. He had a doctor's appointment in New York. As much as I hate that he isn't well, I think he's staying in New York and I'm glad of that," I said. I was surprised that Cade was bothered about my ex-husband showing up in town. He was normally a laid-back person, but Cade had been asking about my ex-husband ever since he arrived in Sparrow a couple of months earlier. We had had a nasty divorce, and I had never wanted to see him again. But then he had suddenly shown up and said he wanted to apologize and to tell me he was dying.

"Good," he said and walked into the living room. "At least we've got the painting done in here." Cade was good at changing the subject.

I frowned. "You don't have to worry about him," I said, joining him in the living room.

"I'm not worried. I think we can get the floors done in here before Christmas," he said, changing the subject back. "We can work on the other rooms later. That way it will look nice in time for Christmas."

"I would love that," I said.

"Where are you going to put the Christmas tree?" he asked, turning toward me.

"Cade Starkey, are you sentimental about Christmas?" I asked, eyeing him.

He smiled with embarrassment. "Not me."

"I think you are. I love Christmas too. It reminds me of everything good about my childhood. Things haven't been the same since my dad died when I was nineteen, and Christmas brings back great family memories."

He nodded. "My mom died when I was sixteen. I hated Christmas for a long time because of the memories it brings back, but I'm looking forward to it this year."

I inhaled deeply. Cade glossed over a lot of things when we talked; his mother's death was one of them. It broke my heart that Christmas had been difficult for him in the past, but it made me happy that he was looking forward to it this year.

I went to him and put my arms around his waist again. "I was thinking about putting the tree right near the front window. That way the lights can be seen from the outside," I said. "And maybe we can put some lights up on the outside of the house. You don't mind ladders, do you?"

"They aren't my favorite, but I can do that," he said, leaning over and kissing the top of my head.

The doorbell rang before I could say anything else.

"I wonder who that could be?" I said and went to the door. I opened it and found my new neighbor standing on the doorstep. "Hello, Ida," I said.

"Hello, Rainey," she said with a smile. "I brought over some pumpkin spice cookies I made. I topped them with buttercream frosting." She held out a plastic Halloween-decorated plate with big cookies that were covered in clear plastic wrap.

"These look delicious," I said. "Thank you so much!" They did look delicious. They were drop cookies that were liberally frosted with buttercream frosting. I could smell the spices through the plastic wrap, and the aroma made my mouth water.

"I put walnuts and raisins in them. I hope you like walnuts and raisins," she said, smiling impishly. "My husband can't stand them, but I add them just to aggravate him."

I chuckled. "I love walnuts and raisins," I assured her. "I'm so glad you brought them by. I know Cade and I will enjoy them."

At the mention of his name, Cade came to the door, and I introduced them.

Ida looked him up and down and gave me a knowing smile. "I'm pleased to meet you," she said to him. "I'm so glad Rainey moved in here. It's been wonderful having her in the neighborhood."

Cade chuckled. "She does brighten up a place, doesn't she?"

Ida nodded. "That she does."

I felt my cheeks go pink. "It's sweet of you to bring the cookies by, Ida."

"It's my pleasure, dear. Well, I should get going. Burt will be wondering where I got off to. You kids enjoy," she said and turned and headed next door.

"Don't keep those to yourself," Cade said as I closed the door.

"I might keep them to myself. They smell wonderful," I said and unwrapped the edge of the plastic wrap so I could wiggle a cookie out. I handed it to Cade and got another for myself. I took a bite and groaned. They were soft and moist and the spices were exactly right.

"Wow, these are good. You've got competition," Cade said, putting the rest of the cookie into his mouth and reaching for another.

"I'd be offended by that, but I can't be. These are awesome," I said. "It's like a fall explosion in my mouth."

I was writing a cookbook with Americana-themed recipes and I wondered if I should ask Ida for the recipe for these cookies. I could give her credit when I published the book. I had a similar recipe, but I thought hers might be better.

Maggie bumped me with her nose and whined for a cookie. "I'll get you one of your cookies, Maggie," I said.

"These are great. I need some milk," he said and headed to the kitchen.

I followed after him. "We better not eat too many. There's going to be some great food at the party tonight. I'll snitch some of these in the middle of the night, though. I'm sure of it." I got one of Maggie's cookies from a jar I kept on the counter and gave it to her. She made it disappear instantly.

"Okay. But I might need to take some home with me," he said, pouring a glass of milk.

"I'll let you. Otherwise, I really will eat way too many of them."

I couldn't wait for the party. It was going to be a lot of fun, and it made the fall season all the more perfect.

Chapter Two

WHEN WE GOT TO THE lodge, a shiny new silver BMW was parked out front. "That's a looker," Cade said as we passed it heading into the lodge.

"It sure is," I said.

There were already a lot of people milling about inside the lodge. After allowing the hot cider punch to simmer and the spices to infuse the juices for a couple of hours, I had poured it into a tightly covered glass container to keep it from spilling and brought the crockpot along to keep it warm. I found a spot on one of the food tables near an outlet and plugged the crockpot in, and then poured the punch back into it. I added more cinnamon sticks and floated thinly sliced apples and oranges on the top. The scent of fruit and spices was bold and sweet, and I inhaled, trying to take it all in. If anyone wanted to turn my punch into an adult beverage, they were going to have to do it themselves. It was perfect the way it was. Cade had brought a bottle of rum to give to the host, Bryan Richards, and I supposed that it would be spiked at some point.

"Wow, this all looks good," Cade said, looking over the food on the table.

One table was dedicated to finger foods, veggie trays, fresh fruit, barbecued little smokies, finger sandwiches, and other tasty things. The next table held main courses of casseroles, German sausages, hamburgers, and the crowning jewel on the table was a whole pig that had spent hours on the barbecue spit. Another table held side dishes, and the last held sweets and desserts. I deposited my pumpkin bread and cranberry bread onto that table. It was enough food to feed a small army, and from the looks of it, that was what we had.

"I agree, everything looks so good. I'm starving," I said as my stomach growled. I had worn a brown chunky knit sweater, jeans, and my brown suede boots. A pair of gloves and a scarf were in my coat pockets for later in the evening when we would go outside to enjoy the bonfire and roast marshmallows.

"Rainey!" Lana Richards called, approaching us with her arms held out. "I'm so glad you could make it."

"Hi, Lana," I said as she gave me a hug. Lana and her husband, Bryan, were the hosts of the event, and their family had been friends with mine for as long as I could remember.

"What a spread, eh?" she said, indicating the tables.

"I've been looking forward to this event for weeks. I missed it when I lived in New York."

"And we missed you. I'm so glad you moved back to Sparrow," she said. Sparrow, Idaho, was a small town that believed in community. To say New York City was the complete opposite was an understatement.

"Thank you, Lana. I brought a hot cider punch, and I put some pumpkin bread and cranberry bread on the dessert table," I said, motioning toward the crockpot.

"You are such a big help, Rainey. I know we'll raise a lot of money for the homeless shelter this year. We need to get as many coats and blankets as we can. I spoke to Farah Simms down at the shelter, and she said they were low on everything."

"I'm sure we'll raise a lot of money. Sparrow residents have always been generous with their giving," I said and turned to Cade. "Lana, this is Detective Cade Starkey."

"I heard about you," she said, shaking his hand and giving him a big smile. "You're still new to Sparrow. We do appreciate your help in finding those responsible for the recent murders. And you're cute as can be. Rainey, good job." She gave me a knowing look and giggled.

Cade smiled. "I try. Rainey's pretty cute too."

"She and her sister are adorable," she said. "Identical twins. Can you believe it?"

I laughed. "It still surprises me sometimes too," I said as my sister Stormy and her husband Bob walked through the door. Stormy and I were thirty-six, but we still occasionally got the "adorable twins" shtick. We were used to it. It came with the twin territory. Stormy was wearing a sweater almost identical to mine and had her long blond hair pulled back into a ponytail. She headed over when she spotted us.

"Hey, everyone," she said. "Fancy meeting you all here."

"And now that you're dressed almost exactly like me, we'll get the identical twin thing all night tonight," I said.

She shrugged and grinned. "Oops! We should have checked wardrobe plans before we came. Bob is putting the cupcakes I made onto the table. Everything looks great."

"You two are so cute!" Lana said, giving Stormy a hug.

"Where are the kids?" I asked Stormy.

"The boys didn't want to come, so I asked them to watch their sisters so Bob and I could have a nice evening out," she said.

"And after a little whining, they agreed it was a great idea," Bob said. "It might have had something to do with my suggestion that they clean the house while we're gone if the girls had come with us."

I laughed. "Poor guys."

"I think it's about time to eat," Lana said. "You all help yourself while I head back to the kitchen and make sure everything is running smoothly."

"Ready?" I said to Cade.

Cade nodded, and as Lana announced to everyone that dinner was ready before heading to the kitchen, we went and got into line.

The offerings on the table were delectable, and I began filling my plate. I was thinking I would need at least three plates to be able to taste everything I wanted from the tables, but I reluctantly decided I would just have to get back in line for seconds instead.

"I don't care what you think, Gina!" a voice shouted above the sound of the crowd.

"Be quiet, Daphne!" someone else hissed.

We all turned to look, and I saw Daphne Richards, Lana and Bryan's daughter, in the middle of the room. Her sister-in-law, Gina Richards, had one hand on her arm and she shook it off roughly.

"I won't be quiet! You can't tell me what to do!"

Daphne was wearing a red sweater that dipped low in the front and tight jeans that looked like she had to squeeze to get into. Her spiky heels made walking difficult as she stumbled, one heel twisting, but she recovered without falling.

I glanced over my shoulder at Cade. He had his eyes on the two women.

"Come on, Daphne, stop embarrassing your parents," Gina said loudly as Daphne headed toward the back of the food line.

"All you've done since you married into this family is cause trouble! You try to split everyone apart, making everyone suspicious of each other. It's like you planned it from the beginning! My brother is an idiot for marrying you!" Daphne said, raising her voice. There was a slight slur to her words, and she almost stumbled again as she continued toward the line that had formed at the food tables.

"Oh, Daphne, stop it! You're such a drama queen," Gina said, rolling her eyes.

I saw Lana head over to her daughter. She took ahold of her arm and whispered in her ear as Daphne made faces. I felt bad for Lana. Daphne had obviously been drinking. Since I had returned to Sparrow, I had heard she had quite a reputation for partying, and I knew she must be embarrassing her mother now.

Daphne shook her mother's hand off and whispered something back. She looked at the crowd of people in line at the food table who were watching her now.

"What?" she shouted and turned and stormed out through a side door.

"Wow," Stormy whispered. "She's gotten worse."

Cade looked at me and I shrugged. We finished filling our plates and found a table to eat at.

"I've got to say, this may be the best spread they've ever put out," Bob said. "Cade, make sure you fill up. There's always great food here."

"Oh, believe me, I will," Cade said, digging into a slice of the pork.

I kept an eye out for Daphne, but she didn't make another appearance. I wondered if she had found some place to sleep it off or had left for another party. If she had left, I hoped she wasn't driving.

The Richards family sat at a nearby table. There were two brothers, Mark and Tim, their parents, and Tim's wife, Gina. The earlier embarrassment of Daphne having been forgotten, they ate and talked happily among themselves.

The food was wonderful, and against my better judgment, I did go back for seconds. I was sad when I couldn't fit any more into my stomach and contemplated whether it would be in bad taste to ask Lana for a to-go container.

"So, after we eat until we can't walk, what do we do next?" Cade asked, sitting back in his chair and sighing, his hands on his stuffed belly.

"We go outside and warm up in front of the bonfire. There will be marshmallows for roasting, s'mores, and maybe a good old fashioned hayride."

"Wow. I haven't been on a hayride since high school," Cade said with a grin.

"Well, it's a lot more fun when you're older. At least I think it is," I said and winked at him.

He chuckled. "I'm up for it. It's a little cold out there, but we can give it a go."

"They usually have blankets we can snuggle under," I promised.

His eyebrows shot up. "That does sound like fun then."

We poured cups of hot cider and went outside. The bonfire was already roaring, and the heat coming off of it felt good in the cold night air.

"Hey, Rainey," Sam Stevens said, walking up to us. He shook hands with Cade. "I'm glad to see you here, Cade. This is an annual tradition in Sparrow." Sam was my boss at the diner and was a great guy.

"Sam, I think I'm going to enjoy this tradition if it means stuffing myself silly with terrific food each year," Cade said.

"It's a requirement," Sam said. The two started talking about football, and I headed over to find Stormy. She and Bob were cozy warm standing next to the fire with cups of cocoa.

"How are things going at your new house?" Bob asked me.

"Great. Cade has been helping out, and it might get finished a lot earlier than I had imagined," I said. I hoped we would be able to get the floors done for Christmas. I could just imagine the tree peeking out from the living room window.

"Hey, it's the Daye Twins," someone said.

Stormy and I turned to look at who had spoken. A tall man with blond hair moved toward us, a grin on his face. It took me a few moments, but I realized it was Alex Stedman. Stormy and I had gone to school with him, and it had been years since I had seen him.

"Alex!" Stormy said.

We greeted one another, and Stormy introduced Alex to everyone. "This is a fun get-together," Alex said. "I haven't been to a fall party since I graduated college."

"You don't live in Sparrow anymore, do you?" I asked him.

"No, I'm in Boise. I own a software company. Stedman Security," he said.

"Wow, you own your own company? I'm impressed," I said. Alex had always been a nice guy, and it was good to hear he was doing well for himself.

He nodded and blushed. "Thanks. It's been a lot of work, but it's the best thing I've ever done. I feel like it's the work I was born to do."

"There's nothing better than getting to do work that you love," I said. I loved cooking, and getting to write another cookbook was something I enjoyed more than anything.

"You can say that again," Alex said.

We visited with Alex for a few minutes before he excused himself and headed back into the lodge.

"I'm so glad Alex has done well for himself," I said to Stormy.

"I said leave me alone! You're an idiot, and I never want to see you around here again!"

The words were slurred, and we turned to look at who was shouting. Daphne was standing on the lodge porch, and she pulled her arm away from a tall red-haired man standing beside her and gave him a light shove.

"I hate you!" She swayed on her feet, a Styrofoam cup in one hand and a cell phone in the other. She turned and headed back into the lodge.

"Daphne!" the man said and followed her back inside.

I turned to Stormy. "Wow. I didn't know Daphne drank that much."

"I've heard rumors that her parents wanted to get her into rehab," Stormy whispered.

I was surprised. I knew Daphne liked to party, but I had no idea she had gotten to the point of needing rehab.

"That's a shame," I said. I hoped she would be able to get some help if things were so bad. She was a smart girl, and it really would be a shame if she didn't get her drinking under control.

"It is," Stormy agreed.

"Who was that guy she was arguing with?" I whispered.

"I'm not sure."

I nodded, hoping Daphne would get her act together before it was too late. We stood around the bonfire, allowing it to warm us up, and discussed fall plans.

"I've got to find the little girls' room," Stormy said after a while and excused herself.

"Bob, how has business been?" I asked in Stormy's absence.

"It's great. Sales have really picked up, and I think there may be a bonus for me coming up soon," he said. "At least, I sure hope so."

"What great news," I told him. "I'm glad things are going so well." Bob had recently taken a job as a realtor. It meant he worked some crazy hours, but he seemed to enjoy the job.

I turned just in time to see Stormy run out of the lodge and head toward us. Her eyes were big, and there was a look of terror on her face.

"Rainey," she hissed. "I think Daphne's dead."

Chapter Three

I STARED AT STORMY, speechless for a moment. When I gathered my wits about me, I said, "Let's get Cade."

I grabbed Stormy's hand like I used to when we were little girls and there was trouble, and we hurried over to where Cade and Sam were still talking sports. They had moved near an outside table set up with beverages and a few other people had joined them. Everyone turned to look at us when we approached.

Bob had followed behind us and Cade took my free hand and drew me to the side. Stormy followed along since I still had her hand, with Bob bringing up the rear.

"What's going on?" Cade whispered when we were out of earshot of the others.

"Stormy found Daphne inside the lodge," I said. I glanced over my shoulder to make sure no one was near enough to hear. "She thinks she's dead."

Stormy nodded, her eyes wide.

"Where is she?" he asked, switching into detective mode.

She took a deep breath. "Down the hallway that leads to the bathrooms. I saw something in the dark, and I went to see what it was. It looks like she was heading toward the storage room that's back there. I checked for a pulse, but I couldn't find one."

He nodded. "You all stay here." He released my hand and heading to the lodge.

But I wasn't staying behind. I couldn't. Cade's long legs ate up the distance to the front porch where he took the stairs two at a time. I hurried after him.

He glanced over his shoulder when he realized he wasn't alone. "Rainey, stay back." He continued on without checking to see if I had listened to him.

My legs weren't long enough to take the stairs two at a time, so I hurried to keep up with him.

"The bathrooms are this way," I said when he headed toward the kitchen. There was a long hallway off the dining room that led to a storage room. Along the hallway were two doors, each leading to a men's or women's bathroom. The far end of the hallway was in the dark, the lights at that end were on a separate switch from the front part of the hallway. I peered into the dark hallway, not at all sure I wanted to go down it.

Cade took hold of my arm at the entrance to the hallway. "Rainey, stay back here. Make sure no one comes down this hallway."

I knew he was trying to keep me from seeing Daphne. That was fine. I didn't need to see another dead body. From where I stood I could see something crumpled in the corner of the hallway near the open storage room door. Cade flipped the light switch on at that end of the hall, and I could see Daphne laying face down. He knelt down and reached out for her neck, trying to find her pulse. After a moment, he pulled his cell phone from his pocket and made a quick phone call, asking for an ambulance. When he had hung up, he turned Daphne over and began chest compressions.

"Rainey," he called to me.

I went to him, trying to keep my eyes off of Daphne.

"Yes?" I said, averting my eyes.

"See if there's a doctor among the guests without letting on to everyone what's happened. I'm sure she's gone, but I want a doctor to call it. Have someone stand at the end of the hallway to keep people out of here."

"I saw Dr. Finley earlier. I'll see if he's still here," I said and headed down the hallway. "Bob, can you make sure no one goes down there?"

Bob nodded, standing at the hallway entrance.

"I couldn't find my phone to call someone. I must have left it in the car," Stormy said, as I headed toward the door. "I couldn't find a pulse."

"It's okay; you did all you could do," I assured her as she followed me.

Once outside, we searched for the doctor, hoping he was still around. We found him getting a cup of cocoa from a table that had been set up with refreshments out near the bonfire.

"Dr. Finley," I said breathlessly. He turned to look at me. "We need your assistance."

The doctor saw the urgency on my face and put his cocoa down and followed me.

"What's going on?" he asked.

"Someone has collapsed inside," I explained. People looked at us as we hurried by, but I ignored them. I didn't want a crowd to gather inside.

I showed him to the hallway, and he hurried to Cade's side and began examining Daphne. We stood at the hallway entrance, and when a woman approached, I asked her to use the bathrooms that were accessible from the outside. It didn't take long before Dr. Finley shook his head and I knew that Daphne really was gone.

"Can you locate Lana and Bryan?" Cade asked me, walking down the hall. "Don't tell them she's dead. Tell them I need to speak to them privately, away from this hallway."

I nodded and headed into the dining room, looking around the room for Lana and Bryan, but only a few stragglers remained in the dining room. Most were out by the bonfire. I headed to the kitchen, pushing open the two swinging doors. Lana was at the kitchen counter, putting candles on a huge white sheet cake that had frosting footballs all over it. When she saw me, she smiled.

"Hi, Rainey, are you all enjoying yourselves? I'm just about ready to bring the cake out," she said, lighting the first of the candles.

"The cake?" I asked, looking again at the cake in front of her.

"It's Bryan's birthday. Sometimes the fall party lands on his birthday, and I like to surprise him with a cake," she said, not looking at me as she continued lighting candles. "I tease him, saying we'll never be able to buy enough candles to put on his cake and that I should get a couple of those number candles instead. But I like when he has to try to blow all the individual candles out."

I swallowed, feeling sick. Bryan's daughter had died on his birthday. When I didn't answer her, she looked up at me, the smile leaving her face.

"Rainey? Is something wrong?"

I swallowed. "Lana, there's been an accident. Cade would like to speak to you and Bryan. Together."

"What kind of accident?" she asked, her brows furrowing as she stood with the propane lighter poised above a blue candle.

"I'm not sure. Someone got hurt," I said, my voice breaking.

"Who?"

"He needs to speak to you and Bryan," I said. "I'll help you."

Her eyes went to the candles on the cake, then back to me again. After a moment, she looked over her shoulder, "Jeff, take care of this cake, please," she said to the cook. She laid the propane lighter down and walked toward me.

"You have an office here, don't you?" I asked.

"Yes, it's off the dining room. What's going on, Rainey?" Worry creased her brow.

I didn't answer her. I didn't want to be the one that told her. "Let's see if we can find Bryan." We headed out the kitchen door.

I could hear the faint sound of sirens in the distance. Stormy stood in the dining room, her arms folded across her chest and her eyes looking misty. Bob had one arm around her shoulders. I nodded at her.

Bryan came into the dining room, concern showing in his eyes. "There's an ambulance coming. What's going on? Is someone sick?"

I nodded. "There's been an accident."

"Are you going to tell me what happened?" Lana asked, her voice shaking now as we stood in the dining room.

I glanced at Stormy, but she looked away.

Cade came into the dining room, worry showing on his own brow.

"There's an office you can use," I said to him and he nodded.

"I wish someone would tell me what's going on here," Lana said, sounding scared.

"Let's use the office," Cade suggested, and Lana led the way with Bryan following behind her.

I turned back to Stormy, thankful it wasn't me who had to tell them their daughter was dead. It might have been selfish, but I didn't have the heart for it. Cade had more experience informing families of lost loved ones than he would like.

People began to come back into the lodge when the ambulance arrived. Bob went to the front door and asked them to stay outside.

Tim and Gina Richards came into the dining room, looking perplexed.

"What's going on?" Gina asked.

"There was an accident," I said. "Cade is talking to Tim's parents in the office. Perhaps you should go in there, Tim."

Tim's eyes got big. "An accident? Is it Daphne?" he asked and headed toward the office without waiting for an answer.

Gina sighed and rolled her eyes, then followed after him. "Drama," she muttered.

After a few more minutes, Cade emerged from the office by himself and headed over to me. He looked worn out, and

I considered how hard it had to be to tell someone that their loved one had died. I reached out and gave him a hug. He allowed it, but I knew he wanted to stay professional while on the job, so I released him quickly.

Four uniformed officers arrived, and Cade led them to the hallway to discuss what had happened.

Daphne had been drinking a lot, but I couldn't understand what had happened. She was young and appeared to be in good health. Had she drunk enough to cause alcohol poisoning? Or maybe she had been unsteady on her feet and fallen, hitting her head?

Chapter Four

"I STILL CAN'T BELIEVE it," Stormy said. We were at our friend Agatha Broome's coffee shop, the British Tea and Coffee Company, sitting at a corner table. Stormy, Agatha, and me, each of us with coffees sitting in front of us. Poor Stormy still hadn't recovered from the shock of seeing Daphne Richards dead on the floor.

Agatha reached her hand out and patted the back of Stormy's hand. "You poor dear. I'm sorry you went through that," she said in her crisp British accent.

We looked up as my mother entered the coffee shop. She smiled when she saw the three of us in the corner and headed in our direction.

"Hello, ladies," Mom said, placing her purse on the floor beneath the table. "Let me get a coffee and I'll join you." She began to turn away, then caught the look on Stormy's face. "What's going on here? Stormy, you look like you just lost your best friend."

"Daphne Richards died at the annual fall party last night," I told her.

"And I found her body," Stormy added, nodding. Her bottom lip trembled for just a second, then she got ahold of herself.

"Daphne's dead? And you found her body?" Mom said, changing her mind and slipping into the empty chair at the table.

Stormy nodded again as her face crumpled. She almost broke into tears, but then she gathered herself again. "I've never seen a dead body before. At least, not one that wasn't at a funeral."

"It was pretty rough," I said to Mom. "I feel terrible for Daphne's family. It was her father's birthday."

"She died on her father's birthday? How terrible. What happened to her?" Mom asked.

"We don't know. She was drinking a lot at the fall party. She did argue with her sister-in-law and some guy, but I think that was due to too much alcohol. Other than that, we didn't notice anything unusual. Everyone was having a good time," I said, filling her in.

"How awful. Dying on her father's birthday is going to make every birthday terrible for the rest of his life," Mom said sadly. "What does Cade say about it?"

"I haven't had a chance to speak to him this morning. He stayed late at the lodge to finish things up, and he hasn't answered my text yet," I said.

"Let me get you a coffee, Mary Ann," Agatha offered, getting to her feet. "The usual?"

"Yes, thank you, Agatha," Mom said. "The poor thing. She was so young. And her poor parents. Losing a daughter that was so young, what a terrible thing." She shook her head.

We looked up as Cade walked through the door. He saw us sitting together, and he gave me a lopsided grin and headed over to us.

"I thought I'd find you here," he said and pulled a chair from the table next to ours and sat down as we scooted over to make room for him.

"What do you know about how Daphne died?" I asked.

"It's far too early to come to any conclusions at this point," he said. He glanced around the table. "We'll get it figured out."

"Did her parents say she had any illnesses?" I asked him.

"No, they said she was healthy as can be," he said.

"Then she was killed? Who would want to kill her?" Stormy asked quietly. "She seemed like a nice girl. Just a regular person." She looked down at her coffee and gave it a stir.

"You never know what's going on in a person's private life," I said.

"Now, hold on you two. It's a little early to jump to that conclusion," Cade warned mildly.

Agatha returned to the table with two cups of coffee. "Good morning, Detective. I've taken the liberty of making a coffee for you as well as my friend, Mary Ann here," she said and set one cup in front of Cade and the other in front of my mother. "I hope I got it right. On the house for both of you."

"That's kind of you, Agatha," he said with a smile. "I could use the pick-me-up. Tell me, did you know Daphne Richards well?"

"She came in here almost every day," Agatha said. "She seemed like a sweet girl. Was it foul play?"

He sighed. "It's possible," he said, glancing at me. "It's a bit premature to know that for sure. Not that we are going to let any of this get around just yet."

She nodded. "I understand. All I really know about Daphne was that she was very competitive in everything she did. She went to the girls' state championship in high school for track. No one could beat her. I think she was also very competitive where her job was concerned. I heard her talking on the phone a couple of times, and she seemed almost obsessed with getting what she wanted. She was in sales. Software, if I remember right."

"She was competitive?" Cade asked, thinking about this. "I suppose a position in sales is commission- or bonus-based and that would make a person competitive."

Agatha nodded. "She was trying to get a contract with a security firm, from the sound of it. There was some sort of software for home security that her company had developed, and there was a large contract at stake. She said another employee with her company was after the very same contract. She was angry. It was a very long conversation that she didn't seem to mind anyone overhearing. I never did find out if she got it or not. I guess I forgot about it until now."

"That's good information to know," Cade said thoughtfully.

"I remember when she was in high school. Seems like there was a write-up in the local newspaper about her nearly every week during the track season, if I remember right," Mom said. "Her parents are such nice people. I sure do feel bad for them."

"They do seem like nice people," Cade said, "It's a shame."

"Competitiveness can get a person in trouble," I pointed out. "Maybe she came up against the wrong person."

Cade leaned back in his chair and took a big sip of his coffee. "Agatha, you make the best cup of coffee in Sparrow."

"Oh, Detective, you make an old woman want to blush," she said as pink crept into her cheeks. Agatha did make the best cup of coffee in Sparrow, and most people knew it. Her coffee shop was always busy.

"Rainey, I might not have any free time to help you with those floors for a while," he remarked.

"I completely understand. I'll try to wait until you do get time. Otherwise, I might rent a sander and see if I can manage it."

"I can come and help you," Stormy offered.

"That would be great," I said. "I'd love to have them done before the holidays if at all possible."

"Then we'll plan on getting some work done later this week. Well, I better get going," Stormy said. "I've got a to-do list a mile long today."

Mom got to her feet along with her. "And I better get back to the flower shop. I hate to leave the girls alone for long."

There was a line at the front counter, and Agatha looked over at it. "I guess I better go help out."

Cade watched them go, then turned to me. "Wow. It's almost like it was planned."

I shrugged. "Great planning then. What's really going on?"

"They're rushing the autopsy. With her being in good health, it looks like it may be poisoning. Some of the employees at the lodge said she was staggering and that she had trouble breathing shortly before she died. One of the employees said she ignored her when she pointed out how hard she was breathing."

"It wasn't from having drunk too much alcohol?" I asked.

"Two of the employees said they didn't think so. One, the dishwasher, said he thought she was acting very strangely. You know they all had to have seen her drunk before, so whatever it was they saw last night, it was different."

"Wow. Any idea what it might have been?" I asked.

He shrugged. "I have no idea, really. They could be mistaken. Maybe she had some sort of health issue that sprang up suddenly."

I thought about it. "She must have been drinking a lot last night. I guess alcohol would disguise the taste of poison?"

"Probably. Especially if she was already drunk by the time it was given to her," he said, "but let's not get ahead of ourselves. We need that autopsy to know for sure."

"That means the killer was at the party," I said, thinking over all the people I saw the night before.

"Most likely. But again, you're rushing things." He looked at me, tilting his head to the side.

I was undaunted. "There must have been over a hundred people at the party by the time things really got going," I observed. "Wouldn't there be something sitting around—a cup or container with the remnants of the poison in it? Oh, and she argued with her sister-in-law and some guy that I didn't know."

"There was a Styrofoam cup in the hallway where we found her. We'll test it and see if it has any residue left in it. Of course, we're just hoping it was her cup," he said. "It's not going to be easy figuring it out, but we'll get to the bottom of it."

"What about her sister-in-law? And that guy?"

"Her sister-in-law says she's innocent, and I haven't talked to a guy," he said with a smirk.

I rolled my eyes. "So you do think it was poison? Whoever did it must have something really big against Daphne. Not just some small grudge, but something big enough for them to plan her death and then carry it out."

He sighed and then nodded. "I agree. If it's murder, they had to have something big against her."

"I guess that's our first order of business then. Find someone that really hated her," I said. "Cade, I'm going to ask around about Daphne, if you don't mind." I really didn't care if he minded. I was going to ask anyway.

He studied me a moment. "You be careful. Don't make anyone mad."

"I won't. People like me. They'll tell me anything."

He sighed and took a sip of his coffee. "Just be careful, Rainey."

"I will. I promise."

Chapter Five

I COULDN'T GET POOR Bryan Richards out of my head. His birthday would forever remind him of the death of his daughter. I did the only thing I could think of and baked a chocolate cake and took it to the family. They probably wouldn't feel like eating, but it would be there if they wanted it later.

Bryan's son Mark Richards answered the door.

"Hello, Mark, I'm so sorry about your sister. I wanted to stop by and see how your family was doing," I said. It felt important to stop by because the Richardses were some of the nicest people in Sparrow.

Mark's face looked drawn and tired. "Thanks, Rainey. I appreciate that. Would you like to come in?"

I nodded and followed him into the house. The Richardses owned a private house that sat behind the lodge. It was an expansive house that had a wrap-around porch and was decorated for fall with pumpkins, Halloween decorations, and a large wreath on the front door. The planters out front had fall flowers in orange, gold, and blue that wouldn't last much longer as the weather turned colder.

"I brought a chocolate cake. I know it isn't much," I offered. It always felt inadequate to bring food to a grieving family, but it was what people did around here and I wasn't going to show up empty-handed.

"That's kind of you, thanks," he said and took the cake from me. "My parents are out right now. Let me put this cake in the kitchen. Would you like some coffee? I made a fresh pot if you'd like to come and get some."

"That would be nice," I said and followed him into the kitchen.

He set the cake on the counter and got cups out of the cupboard. "Cream and sugar?" he asked, handing me a cup. "Help yourself." He indicated the nearly full pot of coffee on the counter.

"Yes, please," I said and poured myself a cup.

He got a carton of cream from the refrigerator and a sugar bowl from the counter and set them on the kitchen table. Then he poured himself a cup of coffee, and we sat at the table.

The tablecloth was a floral print, and cloth napkins sat at each place, ready and waiting.

"Have the police told you anything?" I asked gently, stirring sugar into my coffee.

He shook his head. "They think she might have been murdered. Can you believe that?" he asked, his eyes taking on a glassy look. "I don't know who would do something like that."

"It is hard to believe," I said. "I don't know who would want to do that to poor Daphne."

He poured cream into his cup of coffee and was quiet a moment. "Daphne was always the life of the party. She always had something nice to say to everyone. Always laughing." He shook his head. "But I don't know why they think she was murdered. She didn't have any enemies. Everyone loved her."

"She did have that quality, didn't she? She could make people feel special just by talking to them." It was something I had forgotten about Daphne. When she wasn't drinking, she was a sweet person.

He nodded and looked at me again. "It makes it worse that it happened on my dad's birthday. He'll never celebrate a birthday again. I know him. He will always be reminded of what happened to Daphne."

"That's really a hard one. I wouldn't blame him for not wanting to celebrate his birthday. I wouldn't want to either," I said and took a sip of my coffee.

His hands wrapped around his coffee cup. "Personally, I don't think Daphne was murdered. I think the medical examiner will find out she had some sort of medical defect we weren't aware of. It's not like that detective has the ability to say how she died," he said, looking me in the eye.

"I'm sure he's waiting on the autopsy to know for sure," I said. Cade had been a detective for years, and I thought he had a good eye for details. If he thought there might be foul play involved, then I believed him. But I wasn't going to argue with a grieving man.

"But you know, if someone did kill her, I could take a guess as to who it might have been," he said, still looking at me levelly.

I slowly shook my head. "Who?"

"Jack Farrell. Her ex-boyfriend."

I tried to remember who that was. "I'm not sure if I know him."

"He owns a photography business on Center Street. They were together for a year, but she broke up with him. She said he was pressuring her to marry him and she didn't want to. She said she didn't know if he was the one."

"Was he at the party?" I asked.

He nodded and took another drink of his coffee. "He was the tall redheaded guy. You couldn't miss him."

The mystery of who the guy Daphne was arguing with was solved. Jack Farrell was handsome and stood a good bit over six feet tall. "I did see him. He looked familiar. Is he from Sparrow?"

"No, he moved here a few years ago. He had pestered Daphne to go out with him for at least a year before she finally did. Daphne was seeing someone else. She kept refusing Jack, but he persisted. He was like that. Persistent. When she broke up with her boyfriend, she gave in to Jack."

"Why do you think he would want to kill her?" I asked.

"Because he wanted her back, but she refused to come back to him. She said he turned mean when he didn't get what he wanted, and he wanted her."

I considered this. A bad breakup could have made him want to kill her, but it didn't sound like that was enough motive from what Mark was saying.

"What kind of man is he? Did she say? When things were going well, how did they get along?"

"She said she didn't understand why she stayed with him as long as she did. He could be moody and angry. But most of the time he was fine. I don't know. Maybe I'm jumping to conclusions, but my family has just been torn apart. And whoever is the cause of it needs to be put in jail for a very long time."

I reached out and gave his hand a squeeze. "I don't blame you at all. This is a terrible tragedy for your family to endure. I know the police are looking into it. They'll find the killer."

He gave a curt nod of his head, his cheeks turning bright pink from emotion. "I know the police will do everything they can. I guess there's still a chance that it wasn't murder. Who knows? Maybe she had some sort of deadly allergy that she wasn't aware of?"

The back door opened, and Mark's brother Tim walked into the kitchen. He stopped when he saw me, his eyes red and puffy, and he looked away.

"Hello, Tim," I said gently. "I'm really sorry for your loss."

He looked at me and nodded, but avoided eye contact. "Thanks, Rainey. I can't get over it."

"Mark and I were saying the same thing. You know if me or my family can help in any way, we'll be there for you."

He nodded. "I appreciate that," he said, his voice turning husky. "Excuse me."

I watched as he hurried from the room, and it brought tears to my eyes.

"He's having a hard time of it," Mark said quietly.

"That's completely understandable," I said, blinking back the tears. "So Daphne didn't have any health issues at all?"

"No. Nothing. She was in great shape and she ate right. She was still a runner. It was her sport in high school."

"I remember. How old was she?"

"Twenty-six. I'm twenty-five and my brother is twenty-eight," he said thoughtfully. "We were like the three musketeers when we were kids. We did an awful lot together. Everyone in school knew us. They knew you didn't mess with one of us or the other two would come after you."

"It must have been great being so close," I said. "My sister and I share the same kind of closeness, of course, being twins."

He smiled and nodded. "I can see that."

I took another sip of my coffee. "If there's anything you or your brother or parents need, I'll do my best to help out where I can."

"That's kind of you," he said. "I don't know. I just can't get it out of my head. I really think Jack would be her killer—if she were murdered, that is. I think he had to have planned the whole thing."

"Sometimes your gut is right," I said. "Have you told this to the detective?"

"I did. He said he would question him if the toxicology came back positive," he said.

"I know Cade will find the killer. He's the best detective in the state," I assured him.

He nodded. "I'm sure he is. You know, the other night at the party, I heard Daphne and Jack argue. He said she would give him another chance, or she was going to wish she had." He looked at me, and tears sprang to his eyes. "I heard him. He said it, and I know he meant it because she shook his hand off her arm and told him she would go back to him over her dead body. And now she's dead."

I inhaled deeply. "Wow. And you told this to Cade?"

He hesitated. "I didn't. I don't know why, but all I told him was that Jack was there, and she didn't want to see him. In fact, she had told me two days earlier that she hoped he wouldn't show up and ruin everything."

"That's definitely something to talk to Cade about," I said.

"I guess part of me is still having a hard time processing what happened. And to point the finger at someone to the police, well, I guess it doesn't feel right," he said and exhaled tiredly. "I guess I better learn to accept the fact that she isn't coming back." His voice cracked on the last word.

"I'm sorry, Mark. I really am."

I stayed a few more minutes and then left. It was heartbreaking to think of the Richards family never being the same again after this.

Chapter Six

THE NEXT DAY I DROPPED by Jack Farrell's photography studio. When I walked into the shop, I was greeted by the scent of a burning vanilla candle and wood-framed photos on the wall. Tiny clear lights draped the corners of the room, giving the storefront a warm ambiance.

The store was divided by a short counter that formed a small area with a hallway on the side leading back to what I thought must be the studio. There was a silver bell on the counter and a small placard that said to ring the bell for service. I smiled. It was so small town-like.

Instead of ringing the bell, I looked around at the framed pictures on the wall. I recognized most of the faces from around town. There was Sheila Carnes and Stanley Brewer, a wedding picture for Carla and Mike Smith, and a picture of Sarah James's new baby. Many of the photos were taken at different outdoor sites, but there were a lot of pictures that had obviously been taken in a studio. My breath caught when I saw a small wall display of pictures of Daphne. She was gorgeous. She wore a red sweater that brought out her olive skin tone, jeans, and brown suede high-heeled boots. The pictures had been taken at what looked like one of the local parks earlier in the year. The trees were green and bright beneath the photographer's lens.

"Can I help you?"

I turned around and came face-to-face with Jack Farrell. He was handsome with his red hair and close-cropped beard. He was tall and imposing.

I smiled. "Hi, I was just passing by and thought I'd stop in and take a look around. You do such wonderful work," I said.

"Thank you, I appreciate that," he said, beaming. "I live for photography. It's gratifying to hear someone praise my work."

"I always wanted to learn photography, but I guess I never got the chance. Or maybe I never took the time to learn. My name is Rainey Daye." I reached a hand out and watched his quizzical expression.

"Rainey Daye?" he asked, shaking my hand.

I nodded. "My mother has quite the sense of humor. I have an identical twin sister whose name was Stormy Daye." I rolled my eyes. "Fortunately for Stormy, she got married and changed her last name to Jennings."

He laughed, a deep sound that came from his chest. "Your mother sounds like my kind of woman. I do love a good sense of humor. I'm Jack Farrell."

"Well then, Jack, you'd love her," I said and chuckled.

"Tell me, Rainey, were you looking to hire a photographer?" He looked me up and down, making me feel a little uneasy.

"Maybe. I'm writing a book, and I'll need a new author photo. The one I have is pretty dated. I think it's at least five years old," I said.

He nodded. "It's time for a new one then. What kind of books do you write?"

"Cookbooks. I'm in the middle of writing an Americana-themed cookbook right now."

"Wow, that's exciting. I love to cook. When will your book be published?" he asked, leaning on the nearby wall.

"I think I'll be finished sometime around the beginning of next year. I'm currently sending queries around, looking for a publisher. Hopefully I can get a contract soon."

"So you've been published before?" he asked.

I nodded. "I've had several cookbooks published."

He nodded. "What style picture were you thinking about for your author picture?" he asked. "We can do something formal in the studio, or we can do a casual shot outdoors. There are a lot of beautiful places around Sparrow that we can use as a backdrop."

I turned and looked at a photo of Daphne posed casually beneath a tree. "I kind of like this pose. I like the outdoor shots. They aren't as stuffy as indoor ones." I turned back to look at him.

Jack frowned, his eyes on the picture I had pointed out. "We can arrange something like that. We took that out in the woods near the river."

I turned to the photo, gazing at it. "Did you know Daphne well? It's a terrible shame that she's gone. She was so young." I turned back to him.

He nodded and looked out the front picture window. "We dated for a while," he said, turning back to me. "I don't know how she could have died. She was in great shape. She ran and worked out at the gym."

"I saw her at the gym a lot," I said. "I don't know what happened either. Hopefully they'll figure out soon how she died."

"I heard a rumor that it was poison." He looked at me, as if waiting to see if I would confirm this.

I returned his gaze, wondering who had said that. It made sense that Mark knew there was a possibility of murder since he was a family member, but how did Jack know? Or did he know because he had something to do with her death?

"Poison? How awful. I was there at the party, and she seemed like she had had a lot to drink."

He frowned. "She had been drinking a lot recently. I told her she was going to be sorry. One day she was going to find that she couldn't quit. But she never listened to me. I doubt she listened to anyone."

"She was headstrong, wasn't she?"

He nodded and looked away. When he looked back at me, there were tears in his eyes. "We were going to get back together. We talked about it that night. We were going to go out this weekend."

"Oh, I'm so sorry," I said sympathetically. "Do you mind my asking why you broke up?" Was Mark wrong about Daphne not wanting to be with Jack? Were they really getting back together?

He gave me a sad smile. "Work issues. We both had so much going on. It seemed like it was a good idea to take a break. But as soon as we did, we both knew it wasn't right, and we needed to be together. I missed her so much. She said she really missed being with me. And now she's gone." I could see tears threatening, but he blinked them back.

"I'm so sorry," I said. "I just can't imagine who would do something like that to her, if it's true that she was poisoned. Everyone loved her."

He nodded. "She just had a way about her." After a moment, he took a deep breath. "If you want to know the truth, I think if she was poisoned, it may have been Alex Stedman, her former employer."

"Alex Stedman? Doesn't he own a software company in Boise?" I decided to play it dumb.

He nodded. "That's him. Daphne worked for him for three years. He put pressure on her to date him, but she wasn't interested."

"Really?" I asked. "Her boss wanted to date her? That's kind of crossing a line."

"Like I said, he put a lot of pressure on her. She said he threatened to fire her if she didn't go out with him. I told her to get a lawyer and bring charges against him, but she didn't want to. She said she didn't want to hurt him."

"What difference does it make that it would hurt him? A boss doesn't have any right to pressure an employee to date him." It didn't sound like the Alex I knew back in school, but maybe he had changed.

"That's what I told her. I told her not to be concerned with the consequences her boss might suffer. She shouldn't have been worried about that."

"I don't know," I said. "I think if I was being pressured by my boss, I'd have to get a lawyer."

He nodded. "I told her the same thing. He's the one who was in the wrong. He should have thought of the repercussions before he did what he did."

"I thought I saw Alex at the party," I said, hoping he would keep talking.

He nodded. "He got there early in the evening. I had gone outside, and when I came back in to look for Daphne, he had her cornered in that hallway where she was found," he said. His mouth formed a straight line, and his eyes became hard when he said it.

"I went to school with Alex. I always thought he was a nice guy," I said.

"Like I said, it was early when I saw him. I asked Daphne if she was okay, and he said they were just talking. Daphne went into the ladies' room. After that, I didn't see him again, so maybe he left early," he said.

"Do you know how he might have gotten her to take poison? If that's what happened?" I asked him, not mentioning the fact that I had spoken to Alex shortly before Daphne was found.

He shrugged. "I don't know. I guess she had had a lot to drink. Maybe it was in one of her drinks."

"Did you tell the detective what you saw?"

"I never got the chance to. I heard he was talking to people at the party that night, but I haven't seen him yet."

"I know there were a lot of people at the party. I'm sure he'll stop by. He's very thorough when he investigates."

"You sound like you know him personally," he said.

I smiled. "We're dating."

"Oh? And here I was going to ask you out."

That was the last thing I expected him to say. He had just said he was getting back together with Daphne and how much he missed her. Now he says he wanted to ask me out? He was definitely someone Cade needed to talk to.

"Oh," I said with a chuckle. "Well, we've been dating for a few months."

He nodded. "Maybe if things don't work out, you can give me a call."

I stared at him. "Sure, well, I better get going. I've got to get to work."

I got out of there quick. He had suddenly given me the creeps.

Chapter Seven

"HOW DO SCONES SOUND?" I asked Sam. "More specifically, pumpkin scones?"

He looked over at me. "Well, I like pumpkin anything. At least I think I do. But I've never had a scone before." He turned back to the stove and flipped a row of pancakes he had cooking on the griddle.

I turned and gasped. It was a little dramatic, but someone in this day and age admitting they had never had a scone before was shocking. "Seriously? How can that be?"

He shrugged without looking at me. After flipping the remaining pancakes, he turned around. "I just never had them before. I like simple food, not that fancy stuff."

"Scones are not fancy. We need to rectify this. I cannot allow this calamity to continue. Ron, have you had scones before?" I turned and asked our dishwasher.

"Indeed, I have. I love a good scone with a nice vanilla latte with medium foam," he said without turning around from the sink where he was washing dishes.

I was pretty sure he was teasing me, but I didn't care. Scones were one of my favorite foods, and in honor of fall, they were going to be pumpkin.

The summer tourist season was over. Things were quieter both in Sparrow and at Sam's Diner, where I worked my main job. I got the ingredients out to make the scones. When one of the other waitresses popped into the kitchen, I turned to her. "Dianne, if things get hectic out there, let me know and I'll be right out."

She came over, peering at the empty mixing bowl I had in front of me. "Ooh, what are we going to get to try today?"

"Pumpkin scones. They aren't exactly going to fit in with my cookbook's theme, but I don't care. I've been thinking about making them for days."

"I don't care either. I want some. Make a lot, will you?" she said.

"You bet," I said and began measuring out the flour.

Dianne went out onto the diner floor to wait on customers, and I turned back to the scones.

"So, Sam, what do you think about Daphne Richards's death?" I asked him.

He turned to look at me. "It's a terrible shame. Do you know how she died?"

"The police aren't sure yet. They're doing an autopsy," I said. "Cade said they put a rush on it."

"So he must think it's murder," Sam said. "That's a shame. The Richardses are good people."

"It really is a shame. Do you know them very well?" I asked, measuring out the butter.

"Not really. I did spend the weekend at one of their cabins two weekends ago. Got some fishing in. Steelhead were really biting," he said with a grin.

"Did you see Daphne there?" I asked him.

He nodded and began cracking eggs onto the griddle. "I did. She was arguing with her brother Mark."

"Arguing about what?" I asked.

"I couldn't hear it all, but it sounded like something about a job. I figured it had to do with something that needed to be done around the lodge," he said.

"Did it seem like a big fight?" I asked, measuring out the spices. "Were they really going at it?"

"Sort of. But you know how some siblings can be. It may have sounded terrible, but it might have been just how they usually interacted with each other."

I nodded. "That's true. I'm glad Stormy and I get along so well." Mark had said they were close, but maybe his idea of close was different than mine.

"She was also arguing with her father the next day," he added after a minute.

"What were they arguing about?" I used a can opener on a large can of pumpkin puree.

"Her drinking," he said somberly. "Her father wanted her to go to AA or rehab, and the suggestion made her angry. She screamed at him and told him she would never speak to him again if he didn't drop it."

"I heard her drinking had gotten worse," I said.

"I saw her at a bar a few months ago, and that girl could really put it away. You know she wasn't very big, but it took a while for her to act like she'd had anything to drink," Ron volunteered.

"Really?" I said, turning to him.

He nodded. "It's a shame. A girl that young. She had her whole life in front of her, but it looks like she threw it away by drinking."

Sam looked over his shoulder, but there were only the three of us in the kitchen. "I heard she had a real big problem with it. She got a DUI a few months ago and lost her license. Apparently she had a prior record of DUIs. But you didn't hear that from me."

"Really? I bet that made things hard for her. If she couldn't drive and she wanted to get away from the lodge and buy alcohol, I mean. Sounds like her father wasn't willing to get it for her," I said. It had to have made life difficult for the rest of the family too. From what I knew, Mark still lived with his parents, and his older brother Tim and his wife Gina had a small house there on the property.

"I bet," Sam said. "Did Cade tell you anything about what he thinks happened?"

"No, they're still waiting on toxicology," I said.

"I knew I'd find you in here," Georgia said, standing in the kitchen doorway with her hands on her hips and glaring at me. Georgia Johnson was one of the other waitresses at Sam's.

I looked at her, and it took everything I had in me not to roll my eyes. Georgia and I had a history, and it wasn't a good one. I wasn't even sure why. She didn't like me, and it didn't matter what I did to try to rectify it; she refused to be friends. Or even nice.

"Sam said I could make scones. For all of us. If it gets busy out there, just let me know and I'll come out and help wait on people," I said, looking away.

"Sam?" she said, turning toward him. Apparently, my version of things wasn't going to satisfy her.

"I said it was fine. Just let her know if it gets busy," Sam said without looking at her. I could see his shoulders shake slightly. He might have thought it was funny, but it wasn't funny to me. I was tired of Georgia's attitude toward me.

She snorted and headed over to the order holder, slipping her order onto one of the stainless steel arms. "Funny how some people get away with everything," she grumbled. Before heading back out onto the diner floor, she stopped and rolled her eyes at me.

"I'm not getting away with anything," I mumbled and began mixing the pumpkin into the other ingredients.

She stopped at the kitchen doorway and turned to me. I thought we were about to have a big argument and braced myself.

"You know that Daphne girl everyone is talking about?"

I nodded. "Yeah? What about her?"

"I saw her at a ball game in the spring with her boss, Alex Stedman. They were sitting close together and drinking a couple of beers. I thought it was weird at the time because I heard she was dating Jack Farrell. It just makes you wonder what all she was up to. Maybe dating two different men can get you killed. Especially two men that like to drink." She turned and left the kitchen without another word.

Sam turned and looked at me. "That's a possibility."

"I know Jack Farrell has a history of fighting with people. He has a nasty temper when he's been drinking," Ron said, rinsing a stockpot under the faucet.

"That's certainly something to think about," I said. I needed to get together with Cade. I didn't want to bother him when he was in the beginning of an investigation, but this information might be important. "We're going to have fresh pumpkin scones in just a little while."

"That sounds good," Sam said. "And Rainey?"

"Yes?" I asked, turning to him after putting the mixing bowl onto the stand mixer.

"Don't let it get out that I'm gossiping. Tell Cade what I said if you need to, but I prefer to mind my own business. Most of the time, anyway."

I nodded. "Cade's the only one I intend to tell."

He nodded and plated the eggs and pancakes he had been cooking.

I turned the mixer on. Poor Daphne may have bitten off more than she could chew, and it had ended in her death.

Chapter Eight

THERE WAS A KNOCK ON my door. I turned the heat off under the skillet of pepper steak I was making for dinner and went to see who it was.

"Hey, Cade," I said, smiling when I opened the door. "I was beginning to think I wasn't going to get to see you for a few weeks."

He grinned and shrugged. "I couldn't let that happen. You'd miss my smiling face."

I laughed and stood up on tiptoe to kiss him. "I can't argue with that. Come in. Are you hungry? I was just making dinner," I said and led the way back to the kitchen. I tried not to be a pest when he was busy, but I missed him.

"When am I not hungry? I'd love to stay for dinner," he said. He was dressed in jeans and a T-shirt and looked for all the world like someone's big brother. He looked good in the suits he normally wore, but I liked this look better.

I turned the heat back on under the skillet. I filled him in on what I had learned from Mark and Jack. "So, tell me what's going on. How is the investigation going?"

He shrugged and took a seat at the small kitchen table. "Not a lot. We got a preliminary report of her physical examination back from the medical examiner. He reported that there's every indication that it was a poisoning, and we are conducting our investigation as if it is."

I turned to look at him. "Any ideas what kind of poison?"

"Not yet, we're waiting on the blood screen. But someone wanted her dead, and they got what they wanted," he said, and then a funny look came over his face.

"What?"

He frowned. "You know, I can't remember smelling alcohol on her when I was giving her chest compressions."

I turned the meat over and then looked at him. "What do you mean? She acted like she had a lot to drink. She was arguing with both her sister-in-law and Jack Farrell. It seemed like she was having trouble walking and her words were slurred."

"I know," he said, still thinking. "But I'm sure I would have noticed the smell of alcohol since I was in close proximity to her."

"Like maybe she only had one drink?"

He nodded. "Maybe if it was earlier in the evening, but that wouldn't have been enough to make her behave as if she were drunk."

"From the sound of it, Daphne was a pretty severe alcoholic. I would think having even one drink would be enough to push her over the edge and she'd want to drink more. A lot more."

"I agree with that," he said. "Maybe she wasn't drinking at all. I think it was the poison making her behave erratically, just like the employees at the lodge said."

"Ron White from the diner said he saw her at a bar a few months ago and, for being a small person, she could really put the alcohol away. He said it took a lot of it to have any effect on her," I said.

He nodded. "That doesn't surprise me if she was as severe an alcoholic as people are saying."

"Between you and me, Sam stayed at one of the cabins a couple weekends ago and said she and her brother Mark were fighting. He said it sounded like something about a job. And then the next day she was fighting with her father. He wanted her to go to AA or rehab, and she was mad at him for telling her that."

He considered this for a minute. "I ran a check on her and she recently lost her license due to a DUI."

"Heard that too. If she was stranded at the lodge, maybe she didn't have any alcohol in her system at the party," I pointed out and turned back to the pepper steak. "This is done and we are ready to eat."

"Good, I'm starving," he said, going to the cupboard and taking two plates out. "Her behavior was odd that night. I really thought she had been drinking."

"Me too. If she wasn't, then the logical explanation is that the poison was making her act that way." I took the baked potatoes from the oven and put one on each plate. "Did her parents say much about her drinking?"

"Just that she did too much of it. Her father was so angry about it, he threw out all the alcohol he could find in the house. He also said he threw out the rum I had given him to spike your hot cider punch with."

I chuckled. "Bummer for you."

He shrugged. "I don't drink much, just once in a while. It does make me wonder how she was handling things if she had no access to alcohol."

"So we're back to wondering who spiked her drink and why didn't she taste it," I said and we sat down at the table. Then I remembered the iced tea, and I got up to retrieve the pitcher and put it on the table with two glasses.

"Maybe the poison wasn't strongly flavored. Or maybe someone took advantage of a nice, hot drink at the party. Say, hot cider punch?"

I looked up at him, eyes wide. "No! Don't say someone spiked my cider punch!"

He shrugged. "It had a lot of spices in it, plus the cranberry juice. I think arsenic has a strong fruity taste. It could hide nicely in there."

I sat back in my chair, suddenly feeling sad. "I hope it wasn't put in my cider. I'd hate to have helped a murderer out. Do you think it was arsenic?"

"I don't really know if it was arsenic. And besides, it's not like you actually helped kill her. I mean, you didn't plan it. Right?"

I looked up at him with his cocked eyebrow and the smirk on his lips and narrowed my eyes at him. "Don't you start with that. I had nothing to do with Daphne's murder."

He chuckled and poured some tea into his glass. "You're so easy to tease."

"I'm glad you find that funny. Just get to work finding Daphne's killer."

"I will," he said with a chuckle.

It was stupid to think I had any part in killing Daphne only because the killer had used my punch. But I didn't like the idea of it, no matter how innocent I was.

Chapter Nine

I DROVE OUT TO STEDMAN Security the next day. Seeing Alex Stedman at the party had been a surprise. Finding out Daphne had worked for him was a lucky bonus. I might be able to get some information out of him about Daphne's life and possibly about her death.

"Good morning," the cute blond receptionist said brightly when I walked through the door. She wore dark-framed glasses, and her hair was perfectly straight and went to the middle of her back.

"Good morning, Sydney," I said, glancing at the gold nameplate on the reception desk. "My name is Rainey Daye. I don't have an appointment, but I'm a friend of Alex Stedman's. Do you think you could let him know I'm here and ask him if he has a couple of minutes to see me?" Alex had made himself scarce at the party, disappearing somewhere around the time of Daphne's death. I didn't know if he knew anything about what had happened, but I was going to find out.

"I think he might be in a meeting, but let me message him and see if he's available." She typed something on her computer and a moment later looked up at me with that bright smile. "Isn't the weather lovely out?"

I nodded. "It is. I love the fall, and it's been so nice lately." It hadn't turned too cold yet, and the weather was perfect for working in the yard. The holidays would be here before we knew it, and I was excited about that.

"Alex said for me to show you back," she said, glancing at her computer screen. She got up and led me down a hallway.

The office was bright and modern, its furniture high-end and comfortable. It looked like Alex was doing well for himself.

Alex met us at his office door. He had blond hair and now wore gold-rimmed glasses. He had filled out since high school and was quite handsome now. He smiled. "Thanks, Sydney. Hi, Rainey! It's good to see you again."

"Hi, Alex," I said, and we hugged briefly. "I was in the neighborhood so I thought I'd stop in." He led me into his office and closed the door behind us.

"Have a seat," he said and went behind the desk to sit down. "It was good to see you and Stormy at the party the other night. It's been too long. We need to get together for dinner one night."

I nodded. "We do. I was surprised to see you at the party. Do you get back to Sparrow often?"

"Not as often as I'd like," he said, leaning back in his chair. "But I remembered the annual fall party and thought I'd stop in. It supports a good cause."

I nodded. "It's a shame what happened to Daphne Richards."

He looked at me wide-eyed and shook his head. "It really is Shocking, really, but she did like to party. I can't help but think that she took the drinking too far."

"That may be," I said, nodding. "But I heard it was poison."

"What? What do you mean, poison?" he asked looking at me wide-eyed again.

"Rumors. But I'm also dating the detective on the case," I explained. I thought I might as well come clean about that. He'd met Cade at the party and he'd figure out he was the detective on the case anyway. "Someone poisoned her. They're still waiting on the toxicology report to know exactly what killed her, but they're sure she didn't die of anything natural."

"Wow. That comes as a surprise. I can't imagine who would want to kill her," he said. "She was a nice girl, in spite of her propensity for partying."

"It's terrible, isn't it?" I said. "I seem to remember that she worked here for a while, didn't she?"

He nodded slowly. "She worked here for three years." He looked at me. "To be honest, I had to let her go back in June. Her drinking was getting out of control, and she wasn't completing assignments on time. I hated to do it, but I felt like I didn't have a choice."

"I had heard her drinking was something else," I said, nodding.

"You know how it is. Some people just have a thing for alcohol, and it gets the better of them. It's a shame. She was a bright girl, and I really thought she was going places. I hated to let her go, but I had no choice," he said again.

"It's certainly understandable," I said. "If she couldn't get the job done, you couldn't go on paying her and keeping her on staff."

He nodded. "The funny thing is, her brother applied for a job after I let her go. I interviewed him, but I just didn't feel right about hiring him after letting his sister go."

"Which brother?"

"Mark. He didn't have quite the work experience his sister had though, so that was another reason not to take him on. Still, it bothered me."

I considered this. Daphne might have thought it was a slap in the face for him to apply for the job she had just been fired from. It struck me as odd that he did it too.

"Did you happen to see Daphne and her sister-in-law argue the night of the party?"

He nodded. "I did. Let me tell you something about those two. They were like the proverbial oil and water. They argued all the time. Daphne would come into work on Monday mornings complaining about Gina. They fought all the time, and she said Gina was trying to sabotage the family."

"Sabotage the family how?"

He shrugged. "She said she would pit one family member against another. I don't know all the details. After a while, I kind of tuned it out. Her complaining was pretty excessive. I do remember her saying that Gina would complain that her husband didn't get enough credit for the work he did at the lodge and campgrounds and that infuriated her. Daphne said Gina was afraid he wouldn't get his fair share of the inheritance when their parents died—Gina thought Tim deserved more than either Daphne or Mark."

"Really? I guess the campgrounds, cabins, and lodge have to be worth a pretty penny. They seem to do really well with the tourists."

"I'm sure it's lucrative. To tell you the truth, with the trouble those two seemed to have, it wouldn't surprise me if Gina had something to do with Daphne's murder." He clucked his tongue and shook his head. "I just can't get over the fact that she was murdered. I feel really bad about that."

"It's a shame. She was so young; she had a lot ahead of her," I agreed.

"If I were Cade, I'd keep my eye on Gina. I've heard other things about her," he said knowingly.

"Oh? Like what?" I asked, trying to sound innocent.

"That she's had multiple affairs. She seems to be restless and not very happy in life. She had an affair with another employee at the grocery store when she worked there and broke up his family. I know because he was the brother of a woman I was dating at the time. After his wife left him, Gina left him. She told him she was bored and needed a change. He was pretty devastated. He thought he was in love. It was a shame; he lost his wife and then he lost her," he said and snorted. "Don't get me wrong, it was his fault for getting involved with her. But she just discarded him like he was nothing."

"Well, I'm not sure I'd feel too bad for him since he did have an affair," I pointed out.

"Oh, I agree completely. He should have stayed away from her."

There was a slight smile on his lips and that bothered me. An affair and a broken marriage are nothing to smile about. "Can you think of anything else about Daphne that might be helpful in the investigation?"

His eyebrows furrowed. "Are you helping with the investigation?"

I shrugged. "No, not really. I'm just concerned. My family and Daphne's family have been close for years, and it breaks my heart that she was murdered. I'd like to know who would do something as terrible as murder an innocent girl."

He nodded. "I hear you. I hate to hear that she died, but I don't have a clue, other than that she had a terrible time with her sister-in-law. I'd ask her a question or two, if I were Cade."

He was right. Cade needed to talk to Gina and see what she had to say. It was common knowledge that the two couldn't get along, and with them arguing at the party, she was a prime suspect.

Chapter Ten

AFTER I FINISHED SPEAKING to Alex Stedman, I headed to my second job at the newspaper. I hadn't had the job for very long, but I was enjoying it. I'd gotten to write an article on the new furniture store that had recently opened in Sparrow, another on relationships, and I was currently writing an article on favorite fall dishes. This article was right up my alley, and if I could get enough room in the paper, I was going to add a couple of recipes. I hoped to be able to do this kind of article more often, even though I really did want to expand my repertoire of different types of articles.

I turned on the computer at my desk and waited for the computer to boot up. There were six desks in the front of the newspaper office, three on either side of the room for the writers. There wasn't any privacy, but I found that I had adjusted to it rather quickly. I had the day off from the diner, and it was nice to give my feet a rest from the constant pounding they took there.

I looked up as Karen Forrest walked through the front door. She glanced at me and looked away. She was still a little sore that I had asked her if she had killed her boyfriend, Silas Mills.

Apparently, people don't like that kind of thing. I hoped she would get over it soon because as it was, things were a little chilly when she was around.

When Karen got to her office door, she turned and looked at me and I gave her a smile. She looked away and made a motion like she was going to go into her office, then turned back.

"Rainey, can I see you in my office for a minute?"

My heart jumped in my chest. Karen wasn't exactly my supervisor, but she had been at the newspaper for a long time and had conducted my interview and helped me to get the job. That, of course, was before I asked her if she had killed her boyfriend.

"Sure thing," I said, getting to my feet and following her into her office. The office smelled of vanilla from her favorite candle that she burned most days. She was getting a late start today, but the scent still lingered in the closed room from the previous day.

"So I heard there was another murder," she said casually, going around to the far side of her desk and bending over to put her purse in a bottom drawer.

"Yes, it's so sad. Daphne Richards. Did you know her?"

She nodded and took a seat and then motioned to the chair in front of her desk. I sat down. At least she was trying to be civil to me today. Most days she simply ignored me.

"I guess I kind of knew her. Actually, I really know her parents. But I knew her well enough to say hello to her in passing," she said, reaching down and pushing the button to start her computer. The newspaper was a little behind the times.

She still had one of those behemoth monitors from 2002 on her desk with the computer itself beneath it.

"I guess most people know the Richardses; they've lived here forever," I said. "I still can't believe Daphne's gone."

"Does Cade have any idea what happened?" she asked, eyeing me as she took out a tin of breath mints from her desk drawer and offered me one.

I shook my head to the offer of the mints. "Cade says they only know that she was poisoned. They're still waiting on the toxicology report to know what it was."

She popped a mint into her mouth. "What a shame. I don't know what's become of Sparrow. It used to be such a quiet little town. Things have really been shaken up lately."

"I was just telling Cade the same thing the other day," I said. I wasn't sure what she was getting at here, but I wondered if she had any information on what may have happened to Daphne.

"Can I tell you something?" she leaned forward and asked in a near whisper.

I thought she'd never ask. "Please do," I said, leaning forward.

"A while back I saw Daphne at a bar with her boss, Alex Stedman. I guess that sounds like gossip, but I was so surprised. Wasn't she dating Jack Farrell for a long time?"

"Yes, that's what I heard. I don't know how long they were together, but I think they've been broken up for a while now."

"Oh, then that must explain it," she said thoughtfully and reached around behind her to the credenza and turned on the candle warmer. "They may have already been broken up when I saw her and Alex. My mother and Alex's mother were friends years ago. I can still remember when Alex was born. He was such a cute baby."

"Explain what?" I asked, puzzled.

She shrugged. "I saw them at a table in the corner at the bar. It just seemed kind of, you know, unusual."

"What do you mean unusual?" I wasn't sure what she was getting at here, but I wanted to know exactly what she had in mind.

"It seemed *intimate*," she said, whispering the last word. She nodded her head and looked at her hands as if the word frightened her.

I bit my bottom lip, thinking. "Really? You don't think it could have been just an evening out after work? Sometimes co-workers do that to unwind after a long day."

She shook her head, looking up at me. "No. It didn't seem that way at all. And I guess it was unimportant until she was murdered." She shrugged. "Maybe I'm making more of it than there is. But I saw him reach across and put his hand on hers."

This was interesting. Alex had told me he had fired Daphne, but now they were spending what appeared to be an intimate evening together? Georgia had seen them at a ball game together, but Jack Farrell had said Alex was putting pressure on her to date him. "Can you remember when that was?"

She thought about it a moment and then flipped over the pages of a calendar on her desk. "If I remember right, it was back in April. Silas and I had gone out to celebrate—well, just to celebrate." Her eyes watered at the memory, making me feel sorry again that I had asked her if she had killed Silas.

Alex had said he had let Daphne go in June, and it made me wonder. Had Daphne and Alex had a relationship before she was fired? Why would she have been willingly spending her free time with Alex if he had been pressuring her to date him? It didn't make sense. And if they were actually seeing one another, it would have been a terrible blow for her when he fired her.

"That's something to think about," I said carefully. I didn't want to give away too much. "When I see Cade again, I'll mention it. Alex was at the party the night she died, but so were a lot of other people."

"I don't know Alex well, but I heard he was a ladies' man," she said, nodding. "I suppose that's just gossip, but I heard he cheated on the last two women that he dated."

"Really? I went to school with Alex, and I didn't think he was that kind of person." Alex had always been friendly and open, but I couldn't remember him ever being the flirtatious type. For him to cheat didn't seem to be in his nature. For some reason it made me feel a little defensive. Alex had been a friend at one time.

She shrugged. "Like I said, maybe it's just gossip. Sometimes breakups don't go well, and maybe it's just bitterness coming from those women."

I nodded. Alex always seemed like an upstanding person, and I didn't like the thought of him possibly murdering Daphne. But I hadn't been in contact with Alex for years. People changed, and I really didn't have insight into his life at this point.

"You know how small towns are," I said lightly. "Everybody seems to know something about everyone else. Maybe it was just an innocent evening out."

She nodded, but I don't think she believed it. "Well, I just thought I would mention it. I would hate to keep quiet about it if it ended up being something important."

"I'm glad you told me, Karen," I assured her. "You never can tell when something is important. And it's better to have too much information than not enough."

She nodded and smiled. "Did you hear Gina Richards was opening up a flower shop?"

I stared at her. "No. I hadn't heard that." My mother owned the only flower shop in Sparrow after her business rival had met an untimely demise several months earlier. I hadn't heard so much as a whisper about a new flower shop opening up.

She nodded. "I thought you knew. It's on Fifth Avenue, not two blocks from your mother's shop."

"Really?" I felt the color drain from my face. I probably shouldn't have been surprised that someone would eventually open a flower shop, but for some reason, it shocked me.

She nodded. "I drove by yesterday, and they were hanging the sign up out front. Didn't your mother know about it? Not that it matters. Your mother is the best florist around and everyone loves her."

I nodded numbly. If my mother knew about it, she would have mentioned it. If the new flower shop was on Fifth Avenue, that meant it was around the corner from my mother's shop and she probably never drove down that street. We considered the Richardses to be friends. I would have thought they would have mentioned it at some point, but with Daphne dying, I suppose it was the furthest thing from their minds. But planning a new business would have been in the works for months.

"Maybe she forgot to mention it," I said. "I've been so busy since I moved out of her house and into mine. There's so much to do, I haven't had the time to stop by and visit with her like I should."

She nodded sympathetically. "How's the new article going?" she asked, changing the subject.

"I'll have it finished before I leave today. I was hoping there'd be enough room to run a couple of recipes along with it. I think people would appreciate having them."

"Well, Calvin Hodges is in charge of that so you better ask him. I think it would be a great idea."

I brightened. Writing about food was my specialty. "I'm excited about this job, Karen, and I just can't thank you enough for hiring me on. I owe you one for that." I still wanted to smooth things over so that things would be a little easier between the two of us. I really did like Karen. She lived two doors down from my mother, and I had known her for a long time.

"I'm glad that you're on board," she said, avoiding eye contact. "Well, I don't want to keep you from that article. I'm sure you're eager to get at it."

I got to my feet. "I am really excited about it," I said. "Let me know if you hear anything else, Karen."

I returned to my desk and sat down and texted Cade. I didn't know if what Karen had told me would amount to anything, but I didn't want to be the one who was sitting on information in case it was important.

Chapter Eleven

THE IDEA OF A NEW FLOWER shop in town ate at me the entire time I was at work. I got my article written quickly and added three quick and easy fall recipes, including the fall punch I had made for the party. I came up with the easiest recipes I had that embodied fall and added those to the article. I figured if Calvin Hodges, our editor, didn't like them or didn't have enough room, he could remove them, but I hoped they stayed. It really spruced up the article.

I hadn't bothered texting my mother to ask about the new flower shop. If she knew about it, she would have told me immediately. I didn't think my mother would feel threatened by the competition because she had so many years of experience as a florist. And Karen was right—people really liked my mother, in spite of her sometimes-smart-alecky mouth. But something about the situation didn't sit well with me, and I thought it wouldn't hurt to stop by and see how things were going.

I pulled up and parked in front of the new flower shop. Gina had named it Happy Petals. I sighed. It was cute. I got out of my car and peered in the window. Things weren't quite set up for business yet, but I went to the front door and pushed it open.

Gina was squatted down, wiping the glass front doors of a large refrigerated case. She turned to look when she heard the door open.

She smiled, blond hair shining beneath the fluorescent lights. "Hi, Rainey, how are you today?"

I gave her a smile back. I wasn't going to let on that I was surprised about the shop. "I'm doing great, Gina. How are you?"

"I'm doing wonderfully well. As you can see, I'm getting ready to open for business." She lit up at the mention of the shop.

I nodded. "A new florist shop? I guess Sparrow was due one since The Perfect Flower Shop closed."

"And that was exactly when I decided to open up my shop. I meant to stop by and speak to your mother about it, but things have been so busy. When I told Tim about my idea for the flower shop, he was so excited, you should have seen him. He has helped me so much with this, and we're both ecstatic about this opportunity."

"New businesses are a lot of work," I said, nodding and walking closer to her, looking at the display case she was working on. It looked like it was used but in good condition. "It takes an awful lot of time and energy to get it started, doesn't it?"

"I had no idea how much work this would be," she said and laughed. "But I'm always up for a challenge. This whole thing has been such fun!"

"Gina, how are Bryan and Lana doing? And Mark and Tim?"

She rolled her eyes, catching herself in the middle of it. "Oh, they're fine. You know how it is; they'll grieve for a while but life goes on. They're strong people."

Life goes on? I could hardly believe she had just said that. "Well, it was their only daughter and sister who died," I pointed out.

She snorted. "You know what? That girl was trouble ever since I met her. Her drinking was completely out of control, and she caused her family so much heartache. I'm not saying it's a good thing that she died, because nobody wants that. But you don't know how bad things had been in the family for so long because of her."

"I'm sure addiction causes a lot of problems in families."

"You want to know something else?" she asked, not looking at me.

"What?" I asked, folding my arms across my chest. I didn't know what she had to tell me, but I was pretty sure it wouldn't be nice.

"I wasn't the only one in the family who was tired of her drama." She stood and looked at me, waiting for me to ask who else was tired of Daphne's drama.

"What are you talking about?"

"Mark could hardly stand her. There was so much competition between the two of them," she said. "Family get-togethers were miserable. They were always trying to one-up each other. It was kind of sad and pathetic, if you want to know the truth."

"I'm sorry to hear that," I said with a sigh. Gina was wearing on me. "I can see where things would be hard with her drinking being out of control."

She nodded. "You know that job she had with Alex Stedman?" she asked, turning away from the refrigerated display case. "She took that job away from Mark."

"What do you mean she took that job away from Mark?" Alex had said Mark applied for the job after he let Daphne go.

"What I mean is, Mark had gone down there and interviewed for the job. It looked like Alex Stedman was going to hire him. But when Daphne heard that he was about to be hired on there, she ran down there and sweet-talked her way into Alex Stedman's business. And most likely his personal life, but you didn't hear that from me." She lifted an eyebrow when she said the last part.

I looked at her, taking this in. "Maybe Alex never had any intention of hiring Mark?" Alex had told me Mark applied for a job after Daphne was fired, but he left off the part where Mark had applied for the job in the beginning and hired Daphne instead. Had he applied two different times?

She shook her head. "No way. He'd already made Mark an offer, but he had a business meeting to attend before finishing things up. When he got back from the business trip, he told Mark that there were serious financial considerations and he would be unable to hire anyone at that point. A month later he hired Daphne."

I looked at her wide-eyed. "Well, that would really stink, wouldn't it? Losing out on a job only to have your sister hired for the same position you thought you were going to get."

She nodded. "You better believe it. When Mark found out, he was livid. He wouldn't speak to Daphne for six months, and the only reason he began speaking to her again was because their silence tore his parents up. Lana and Bryan hated to see any kind of trouble between the kids, but they sure didn't try to stop the trouble when it was Daphne who started it."

If what Gina was saying about Daphne was true, I could see the ways in which life in that family had to have been pretty miserable. "That's a real shame. It really would make life difficult having to live with that kind of thing."

She nodded. "I don't know why Bryan and Lana put up with her shenanigans like they did. Honestly, if they would have put their foot down earlier in Daphne's life, she might still be alive now. Her drinking might not have been so completely out of control."

"What do you mean?" I asked her. It seemed like Gina jumped to conclusions quickly. She'd be a real peach to be around for any length of time.

"They spoiled her. Being the only girl, and especially being daddy's little girl, she got whatever she wanted. You would've thought that with Mark being the baby in the family, it would have been him to get all the attention. But it wasn't; it was Daphne. She got away with anything she wanted. When we were in school, she was constantly being called into the principal's office because she had no respect for authority and was always disrupting class. Of course her parents shrugged it off. Daphne never got into trouble."

"That sounds like a nightmare," I said.

"That's exactly the word for it. Look, it's not like I didn't like Daphne. She had her moments. One time, right after Tim and I got married, I had made a really big mistake when I was paying our bills. I was a newlywed and had never had the responsibility of balancing the checkbook and making sure the bills were paid, and somehow I messed up my checkbook. Well, I told Daphne what I had done, and she loaned me fifteen hundred dollars so the checks wouldn't bounce."

"That's really nice of her, considering you all didn't get along well," I said.

She shrugged. "She could be nice when she wanted to be. And it's not like I enjoyed not getting along with her. I would have loved to have had her be my friend, but all she did was stir up trouble."

"What a shame that everybody couldn't get along," I observed, hoping she would go on. She was moving right up the ranks of people I thought might have killed Daphne.

She nodded. "You want to know something else? She got me fired from my job at the grocery store. She went and told the manager that I was rude to her, without telling him that she was my sister-in-law."

"Really? Didn't the manager ask for her name?"

"She gave him a phony one. After I got fired, she told me what she had done and laughed about it," she said. Her cheeks turned pink as she spoke, and I thought that Gina probably hadn't forgiven Daphne for what she had done. But I did have to wonder why a store manager would fire an employee with just one complaint.

"So how was your job going before she did that? I mean, were there other complaints?"

She narrowed her eyes at me. "No, I didn't have any other complaints against me. But I was still in my ninety-day probationary period. And that manager, let's just say he was known for being a jerk. From what the other employees told me, he loved to write people up, and if he got the chance to fire someone, he jumped on it. And of course, since I was still on probation, I was easy pickings."

I nodded. "I'm sorry that happened," I said. I wondered if things really happened the way she was saying they did. It seemed extreme that anyone, even a bad boss, would just fire someone from one complaint, especially when that complaint had come from someone whose identification he hadn't even gotten.

"Well, I better get back to work. I've got so many plans and so much to do," she said shrugging and smiling again, having recovered from her anger at the memory of Daphne's betrayal.

"When are you going to open the shop?" I asked.

"It'll probably be at least a month. I had hoped to be open sooner than this, but Tim's parents wouldn't loan us the money at first." She rolled her eyes. "If it had been Daphne asking for the money, you can bet they'd have ponied it up real fast."

"Opening a new business is expensive," I agreed.

"Yeah, it is. But we finally got them to see things our way. Sparrow needs another flower shop, and I have so many great ideas. At least we'll be open before Christmas."

"The Christmas season is an important time of year for a flower shop to be open," I said, pushing down the feelings of resentment. I knew I had nothing to worry about where my mom was concerned, but the fact was, I was annoyed about the prospect of another flower shop opening up.

We talked for a few more minutes and then I left. Gina left me with more questions than answers. All she had done was complain about Daphne and her family, and it made me wonder about her. Tim's parents had come up with the money for the new business but only after Gina had worked on them for a while. It took a lot of nerve to pester your in-laws for money they didn't want to give. It made me wonder if some of that family trouble she talked about was because of her own actions and had nothing to do with Daphne.

Chapter Twelve

"WHAT HAVE YOU GOT FOR us today, Rainey?" Sam asked as I pulled a pan out of the oven. "I smell cinnamon."

I set the cake pan on a rack, inhaling the wonderful scent of cinnamon and nutmeg. "You got it right. Cinnamon, plus a liberal dose of nutmeg. I made a cinnamon crumb cake."

He turned to look at me. "Cinnamon crumb cake? Something about that sounds familiar."

I couldn't help but grin. I had recently had a run-in with a killer that had issues baking cinnamon crumb cake. "Yeah well, I was left frustrated with the quality of the one I tasted not long ago, so I decided the only remedy was to make one of my own. It's a classic fall favorite, you know."

He chuckled. "Sure does smell good," he said and turned back to the grill. "I'd eat that any time of year."

"I'll let this cool off before cutting into it. I have to get back out front and see if there's anyone new at the front counter," I said and laid down the oven mitts. When I got back out front, my mother was sitting at the front counter. I hesitated. I hadn't told her about the new flower shop; I was still trying to process the whole idea that Gina was opening one up.

"Good morning, Rainey," she said, pursing her lips. "I've been waiting out here forever."

"Now you know I'm not going to believe that," I said, pulling my order book from my apron pocket. "I was only in the kitchen for a couple of minutes. What would you like this morning?"

"Do I smell cinnamon?" she asked, peering at the kitchen pass-through.

"I made a cinnamon crumb cake, but it's too hot to serve. I just took it out of the oven," I said.

"Well get me a cup of coffee, and I'll wait until it cools down enough that you can cut me a piece. It smells too good to pass up."

I raised one eyebrow at her. "Cake for breakfast? That's not exactly the breakfast of champions. If it were me, you'd tell me to eat some protein."

She shrugged. "I'm old enough to make my own decisions, you know."

I chuckled and got her a cup of coffee and brought it back, setting it in front of her. "Mom, did you know that there's a new flower shop opening?"

She looked up at me as she reached for the sugar. "I heard a rumor, but I haven't had time to check into it. So it's true?"

I thought that was odd. My mother was the nosiest person I knew. "Really? You didn't check into it? I would have thought you would have been all over that. Gina Richards is opening it up right around the corner from your shop."

Her eyes went wide. "Right around the corner? How right around the corner?"

I nodded. "Two blocks away, on Fifth Avenue."

She poured sugar and creamer into her coffee while she thought about this. "Well, Lana didn't tell me they were planning on opening a new business. I just spoke to her two days ago."

I could tell she was bothered by the news. "I would imagine she's got her mind on Daphne," I said softly. "I spoke to Gina for a few minutes yesterday. She seems very bitter toward just about everyone in that family."

She looked up at me. "I always had that impression about her. If you want to know the truth, I think she worries Lana terribly. I remember last year when she came in to buy flowers for Gina's birthday. She told me she felt she had to spend a lot of money on a big arrangement, otherwise Gina would disapprove and cause trouble in the family. She spent a hundred and fifty dollars on flowers for her."

"Wow. Nothing like making sure the person buying you a gift knows they need to spend a lot of money on you or else," I said. A hundred and fifty dollars was a lot of money to spend on flowers, especially since it was for her daughter-in-law and not someone closer to her.

She nodded. "Lana nearly broke down in tears as she looked through the book. I asked her if everything was okay, and she just shook her head and was quiet for a few minutes. I didn't want to push her, so I waited."

"She was that upset?" I asked.

She nodded. "She said Gina and Daphne fought all the time. The two of them couldn't be in a room without one or the other being hateful. She said holidays were bad. It seemed to bring out the worst in both girls."

What she said didn't surprise me at all. From what Gina had said the day before and from what I had observed between Gina and Daphne on the night of the party, I believed every word of it.

"Poor Lana and Bryan," I said, still holding my order book. "It's a shame Daphne died on her father's birthday."

She nodded and took a sip of her coffee.

The diner door opened, and Cade walked through it. He stopped and gave me a big smile, heading to the front counter and taking a seat next to my mother. "Ladies, how are we this morning?" he asked brightly.

"We are doing just fine," Mom said as she reached over and gave his hand a squeeze. "Have I mentioned how glad I am that you're dating my daughter? I was so worried about her being alone for the rest of her life. But here you are, my knight in shining armor, rescuing me from having to take care of her in her middle-age."

I rolled my eyes as Cade chuckled. "Well, Mary Ann, I'm glad to be of service to you. It's what I live for."

"Oh I'm sure it is," I said, rolling my eyes again. The two of them could go on a comedy tour. "Scrambled eggs and white toast?"

He nodded. "That's what I like. I don't have to explain myself; you already know what I want."

"It's not exactly creative, now is it?" I said and jotted down his order and headed to the kitchen to turn it in to Sam.

Georgia gave me the evil eye as I passed her. I decided to just ignore her. Daphne and Gina may have had their issues, but they weren't the only ones with issues.

"I heard something about Daphne," Georgia said, following me into the kitchen. "She was driving drunk one night and nearly killed a woman crossing the street."

"Tell me something I don't already know," I said and went to the crumb cake. It was probably still too hot to cut, but I picked up a sharp knife and decided I'd give it a shot anyway. I was careful with the knife and then used a cake server to hold the piece together and cut one for both my mom and Cade. Cade loved his sweets and I knew it would be a nice surprise on a cold morning. It smelled wonderful and I couldn't wait to try it myself.

"I think whoever killed her did the town a favor. She was dangerous."

I don't know why Georgia suddenly wanted to make conversation with me. She couldn't stand me. "Well I guess she won't be a menace to pedestrians anymore." I picked up the plates and headed back out to Mom and Cade.

"Your mother's telling me there's going to be a new florist shop in town," Cade said as I set the cake in front of him. His eyes went to the cake. "What is this?"

I poured him a cup of coffee and set it down in front of him. "Cinnamon crumb cake. I have it on good authority that it isn't dry and overcooked."

He stirred sugar into his coffee and kept an eye on the piece of cake. "I hope the new florist shop isn't going to hurt your business," he said to Mom.

She shrugged, "I hope not either. But I've been in business in Sparrow for a lot of years. I'm not worried about a thing." Mom's words were confident, but I heard a hint of doubt in her tone. I thought Mom's business would be fine. If she was worrying, it was for nothing.

"What do you know about the murder?" I asked Cade, lowering my voice.

"We have a dead woman on our hands," he said with a smirk.

I groaned. "I heard she had a problem with her younger brother," I informed him.

He looked at me with interest, eyebrows raised. "Oh?"

I nodded. "According to Gina Richards, Daphne's brother Mark just about had a job at Stedman Security, but when Daphne heard about it, she supposedly went and turned the charm on to Alex Stedman and swooped that job right out from underneath her brother."

"If that's true, then I'm sure there was a whole lot of uncomfortable moments at family get-togethers," he said thoughtfully.

"You can say that again," I said. "But Gina is very bitter toward not only Daphne but everyone in that family other than her husband. Could be she's exaggerating."

"Want to hear something funny?" he said, taking a drink of his coffee, then set the cup back down.

I nodded, leaning on the front counter.

He looked over his shoulder and then back at me. "We got some of the labs back on some items that were removed from the lodge. Remember the Styrofoam cup? It had aconitine in it, along with a trace of cyanide."

"I know what cyanide is. But aconitine?" I asked. "What's that?"

"Wolfsbane. It's a flower that is deadly, causing an unsteady gait, slurring of speech, unconsciousness, and if given in high doses, death," he said.

"Why would Daphne eat that? Or drink it?" I asked, glancing at my mother who was all ears.

"It can be dried and ground into a powder and put into capsules. It's rather common and grows naturally in North America," he said.

"Wow," I said, taking this in. "And what about the cyanide?"

He shrugged. "Cyanide occurs in a lot of places naturally, and we aren't sure yet if what we found was in a large enough concentration to kill her."

"But it could have been the combination of the two?" I asked.

He nodded. "It could have been. But what's more interesting is that the Styrofoam cup also had traces of apple juice, cranberry juice, cloves, cinnamon, and other spices in it."

I stared at him, straightening up again. "My punch?"

He nodded. "The one and only."

"Rainey, you have some explaining to do," Mom said sternly. "Didn't I teach you better than to poison people?"

I narrowed my eyes at her. Someone might think I did have some explaining to do. I had just written an article with the cider punch recipe and it was set to run in today's newspaper. Sans poison, of course.

Chapter Thirteen

I COULDN'T GET OVER what Cade had said earlier in the morning. My fall cider punch had been used to poison Daphne. I knew no one was going to try and pin the murder on me, or at least I didn't think they would. But it was sinister—the idea of someone using something as tasty as my punch to kill poor Daphne.

Right after Cade had told me about the punch, things had picked up at the diner. I didn't get a chance to speak to him about anything else, but we were going to meet later in the evening for dinner. As soon as my shift ended at the diner, I went out to visit Lana at her home. I hoped she had something new to tell me that might help in finding Daphne's killer.

Lana opened the door, and I could see the toll Daphne's death was taking on her. My heart went out to her, and I resolved to do everything I could to help Cade find the killer as soon as possible.

"Hello, Rainey," Lana said quietly. "Would you like to come in?"

I nodded. "How are you holding up, Lana?" I followed her into the living room and took a seat next to her on the sofa.

"Oh, you know how it is. I'm doing the best I can. Poor Bryan though, he just can't get over the fact that our little girl is gone." Her voice cracked on the last word.

I reached over and squeezed her hand. "That's completely understandable. You all have suffered a tremendous loss."

She looked at me, her eyes tearing up. "This isn't what you picture happening to your family. This thing has got us all in a mess."

"I'm so sorry. It just breaks my heart that you're going through this."

She blinked away the unshed tears. "Poor Tim is having a terrible time with this. His wife Gina has been down at the new shop and doesn't seem to care what her husband is going through," she said, and then her eyes got big. "Oh my goodness, did you even know about the flower shop that Gina is opening? Does your mother know? I told Gina to go over and discuss it with her, but I bet she never did."

I nodded. "I heard about it yesterday. You all must be excited for her." I forced myself to smile. I didn't want her to think I was upset about it. She had enough on her plate.

Her mouth formed a hard line. "I don't think excited is the word for it."

I sensed there was trouble where this flower shop was concerned. "No?" I said and left it at that.

She shook her head. "I don't mean to complain, but I was completely against loaning her the money for the flower shop. Especially after I learned that everything was in her name, and Tim wasn't really going to have anything to do with it."

That seemed odd to me. Tim and Gina had been married for more than ten years, and I couldn't imagine why they wouldn't go into business together. When we had talked, she acted like he was as much a part of the flower shop as she was. "Oh? Tim isn't going to help with it?"

She shook her head again. "She insisted that he had enough to do here at the lodge. And that's true, we do rely on him for an awful lot around here. If it weren't for him, Bryan would be working himself to the bone. But Tim is such a big help and sure has made things easier around here."

"I always thought he was a good worker," I agreed. I had only heard good things about Tim for as long as I could remember. He was quiet and a good guy, always pleasant to talk to.

"Tim has always been a hard worker. I've always been so proud of him," she said and looked away. "I told Gina she needed to speak to your mother about the flower shop. Just to give her a heads up. I can imagine this is a shock to her. I sort of feel like I've betrayed her just a bit." She looked down at her hands.

"Don't you worry about my mother. She understands you're going through a lot right now and that the flower shop is the last thing on your mind."

She looked up at me again. "That Gina is something else. All she does is complain about everything Tim does, and of course, Daphne could never get along with her."

"Sometimes different personalities clash," I said, hoping she would elaborate.

She chuckled bitterly. "You can say that again. Now look at me, sitting here complaining about somebody else complaining.

I'm a piece of work, aren't I?" she said and laughed a genuine laugh this time.

"Lana, you've been through so much that I wouldn't blame you for anything you said or did."

She looked at me again. "You don't know how much I appreciate hearing you say that. I think I listen to what Gina says more than I should, and I guess I take her criticism to heart. It's just a breath of fresh air to hear you say something that sweet."

I shouldn't have been surprised, but I was. Was Gina always as negative as she had been the day before? I would have thought she would at least try and hold back some of the vitriol.

"You should never take other people's criticisms to heart. You never know what it actually stems from, and some people are just negative people."

"You're right. I need to learn to ignore her, don't I?" she said.

I nodded. "Lana, what happened to Daphne's job? Didn't she work for Stedman Security?" I asked.

She nodded. "She was laid off. She said her boss was having financial trouble and had to cut back staff. It was a shame. Daphne really liked it there."

I tried not to let the surprise show on my face. It made sense that Daphne wouldn't tell her mother the truth about her job. "I guess there's not much you can do if a company is struggling and lays you off. I bet she was disappointed if she loved the job."

"She was. She moped around for weeks. To make matters worse, she had just bought a new car. Bryan and I helped her out with the payments; we couldn't let her lose the car. Getting laid off wasn't her fault."

We both looked up when the front door opened and Mark walked in. He stopped, looking surprised to see me, and then smiled. "Hi, Rainey," he said and walked all the way into the living room. "How are you doing?"

"I'm fine. How are you, Mark? I was just in the neighborhood and decided to stop by and see how you all were."

He nodded and smiled. "I guess we're doing as well as can be expected. With Daphne gone, there's just a hole left in our lives."

"Poor Mark has been so distraught over this," his mother said.

"I can imagine. I'm sure the police will find the killer soon," I said.

"I just don't understand a crime like this. Who in their right mind would kill a person? I can't wrap my mind around it," Mark said, shaking his head. I wasn't sure if either of them knew that my punch had been used to give the poison to Daphne, and I didn't want to volunteer the information.

"I know the police are working on it. Cade has been putting a lot of long hours in," I assured him.

"Yeah, I don't think he has that far to look, if you want to know the truth," Mark said bitterly.

I looked at him wide-eyed. Had he heard about the punch? Certainly he didn't blame me, did he? "Oh? What do you mean by that?"

He glanced at his mother, and she gave a slight shake of her head. "My mother doesn't want me to say anything, but I know the truth. It was Gina. She's the most bitter, hateful, spiteful person I've ever met in my entire life." His face turned red, and he clenched his fists at his side.

"Now, Mark," Lana said softly. "We need to be more understanding of others. You know she had a rough upbringing and has a hard time dealing with people."

I didn't know anything about Gina's upbringing, and now I wondered about it. Was there a reason Gina was so bitter?

"You always say that, Mom," Mark said and slumped down in the chair across from the couch we were sitting on. "But I've had just about enough of being understanding about her attitude. She's been nothing but hateful since she joined this family. It's like she resents all of us for something that we didn't do."

Lana's lower lip trembled for just a couple of seconds, then she recovered. "I know, but some things just can't be changed," she said and turned to me. "I don't know if you know it, but Gina had a rough childhood. When her parents got a divorce, she ended up in a foster home for nine months. Gina doesn't say a lot about it other than it was pure hell. That just breaks my heart. A little nine-year-old girl going through whatever it was that she went through."

That might explain things, I thought. Gina may still be bitter over what she went through as a child and now it was spilling out in her frustrations with Daphne. "I'm sorry to hear that," I said. "But I can kind of see Mark's viewpoint. She shouldn't take her anger out on the rest of the family. Have you suggested she get some kind of help?"

"Yes, we've all suggested it. Tim has begged her to go to a therapist, but she refuses, saying she's fine."

"She can get all the therapy she wants once she's put away in prison for life," Mark said bitterly. "Personally, I don't care one way or another about her. I know what she did, and she is going to have to pay for her crime."

"Have you discussed what you know with Cade?" I asked him.

He nodded. "I talked to him about it. But he insists that until there's some kind of evidence, there isn't much he can do. And I understand that, but I'm telling you, I know Gina killed my sister."

At this point, after all I'd heard, it wouldn't have surprised me if Gina did kill Daphne. But I agreed with Cade. Until there was some real evidence, there wasn't much he was going to be able to do. We would just have to wait until Cade could come up with more proof. I decided I wouldn't bring up the issue of the punch if Cade hadn't already told them. No use muddying the waters.

Chapter Fourteen

"WHAT ARE YOU GOING to order?" I asked Cade as I looked over the menu. We were at a little steakhouse out on the highway about halfway to Boise. It was an out-of-the-way place that people came to from miles around. It gave off a real country vibe that was kind of fun and very casual.

"I'm staring down a T-bone steak right now," he said without looking up. "Are they good here?" He was wearing a T-shirt and jeans, and in spite of the fact that he normally wore business suits, he looked like he fit right in.

"Everything they serve here is good. Very good," I said. "I think I'm going to go with the avocado bacon burger. I'm in the mood for avocado and bacon, in case you couldn't tell."

He nodded and chuckled. "Wise choice."

The waitress brought out our drinks we had previously ordered and then took our food order. When she left, we sat and just looked at one another. It was all I could do to keep from giggling. I finally had Cade to myself for a few hours.

"Okay, I want to hear it. What do you know?" I finally said.

He chuckled, "Aren't you going to give me a minute to relax? Sometimes I think you only want me around for my murder case information."

"You relaxed on the way over here," I said. "I thought I showed an awful lot of self-control by not grilling you while in the car."

He chuckled again. "I guess I have to give you bonus points for that. I already told you about the Styrofoam cup with the punch, your punch that most likely covered up the taste of the poison nicely, and I've questioned most people of interest."

"Stop bringing up that it was my punch that was used to cover up the taste of the poison," I said.

He grinned. "I'm just sticking with the facts."

I raised an eyebrow. "Fingerprints?"

He shrugged. "We couldn't get anything besides Daphne's and a few smeared prints off of the cup."

"What else?"

"I have my feelers out right now, and I'm feeling that Jack Farrell is a suspicious character."

I nodded. "That wouldn't surprise me. But I talked to Lana and Mark Richards, and they feel very strongly that it may be Gina Richards who did it. And I have to tell you, I've got a really strong feeling about her. She's incredibly bitter and angry. It sounds like she and Daphne argued all the time."

"She is a bitter person, isn't she? She was spewing a lot of venom when I talked to her," he said. "But here's something that you may not know. Jack knows how to get ahold of cyanide."

I looked at him. "How?"

"Jack still likes to develop pictures the old-school way. Those sepia-tone prints require a chemical mixture that includes cyanide. He claims he doesn't want to use software to duplicate the effects of sepia-tone pictures and that he likes creating the real thing."

I sat back and thought about this. "So did you ask him about it? About the cyanide?"

He shook his head. "I just found out about it this afternoon when it came up in casual conversation with another detective in Boise. Seems he's a photo buff himself. I will be going back to ask Jack about it tomorrow."

"Interesting," I said carefully. I picked up my iced tea and took a sip and put it back on the table. "But what about the other poison? The wolfsbane? How would he get ahold of it?"

"Health food store."

I stared at him a moment. "Health food store?"

He nodded. "It's easy to get ahold of. You can grow it in your garden if you want, but I wouldn't recommend it."

I took this in. "And if it's not Jack, what about Daphne? How are you going to be able to prove that she did or didn't do it?"

"Since there isn't a lot of evidence at this point, there's not a lot we can do except wait and see if she, or somebody else, trips up and maybe admits to something, or we find more evidence."

"Let's hope that happens quickly," I said. "Bryan and Lana are such nice people, and I hate that they're going through this."

He nodded. "What about that flower shop that Gina is opening up? Did you talk to them about it? I think your mother is more bothered by it than she's letting on."

I nodded, "I do too. Lana is not happy about it. Apparently, Gina put a lot of pressure on them to loan her the money. They weren't going to do it at first, but it sounds like she pressured them into it. After they gave her the money, they found out that Tim wasn't going to be involved in the business and nothing was going to be in his name."

His eyebrows raised in surprise. "Really? Did they find this out afterward? I can see where that would make them angry."

I nodded. "It would make me darned angry too, especially since she put a lot of pressure on them. Gina is bitter and angry toward them for some reason. Lana said Gina spent time in it a foster home when she was nine, and she thinks that's where it stems from."

"So she's taking out her anger on them? Maybe because they're all such a happy family?" he asked and picked up his water and took a drink.

"That's what Mark seems to think," I said. I picked up my glass of iced tea again and then stopped. "Wait, a minute. Maybe Gina bought some wolfsbane for the flower shop."

He grinned. "That would be one deadly delivery for someone. It is a beautiful purple flower, but I doubt you could order it through a legitimate florist supplier."

He was right, of course, but it gave me chills thinking that she had access to all sorts of plants and that it was at least part of what killed Daphne. "One more reason to look at her closely," I said.

He sat back in his chair and looked around. "This is a busy place on a Saturday night."

"It's a busy night every night," I said. "I can't believe you didn't know about this place while you lived in Boise."

He shrugged. "There are a lot of nice places in Boise to eat, and I guess I just hadn't traveled out in this direction before."

"You've lived such a sheltered life," I teased.

"That I have," he said. "How about next weekend you rent a sander for your floors? It'll probably take me a while to get them finished, but maybe if I work on them a little every evening, we can get it done before the holidays."

I got excited. "Really? That makes you the best boyfriend ever!"

He shook his head and laughed. "Don't you ever forget that, either."

I sat back in my seat and smiled to myself. If Cade hadn't been persistent in asking me out, I never would have said yes. I didn't trust him at first, but I was glad I finally had. And as much as I hated to admit it, if my ex-husband hadn't shown up in Sparrow and made peace with me, I never would have been able to move beyond my failed marriage.

Chapter Fifteen

THE DAY OF DAPHNE'S funeral dawned dark and gloomy. It matched my mood. Mom, Stormy, and I went together for support.

The Baptist church was filled to capacity, with people milling about before the service. I looked around and saw so many familiar faces. Daphne would be sorely missed by a lot of people.

Mom reached over and squeezed my hand, and when I looked at her, she nodded at the open casket at the front of the church. I didn't want to see Daphne, but I knew we had to pay our respects, so the three of us headed down the aisle of the church.

When we got to the casket, I looked in at Daphne, who looked just as beautiful in death as she had in life. It broke my heart even more. She had had so much potential, and it had been wasted.

"Poor thing," Mom murmured.

"I can't believe she's gone. She was so young," Stormy said.

Lying in that coffin, Daphne's youth and beauty were wasted. I shook my head sadly. It just didn't seem possible. After a few moments we turned around and came face-to-face with Daphne's grieving family on the front pew. I hesitated as Lana and Bryan sat stoically on the pew, not making eye contact with anyone. Mom took my hand and led me back up the aisle. There would be time for paying our respects to them after the funeral.

We sat at the back of the room, squeezing in next to the Oliver family on the last pew. This gave me an opportunity to see who all had shown up. Would the killer be here? I thought they just might be.

Sometimes the atmosphere at a funeral can be one of restrained happiness. Not that anyone is happy that someone has died, but the person being celebrated brought such happiness into other people's lives and there's the knowledge that they had lived life to the fullest. But when someone young dies, it's a different situation. The atmosphere at the church was subdued. Everywhere I looked, I saw tears and sadness. And that was the way it should be. People who were young shouldn't have their lives cut short. They should go on to marry, have children, and fulfill whatever purpose they were put on this earth for.

"I don't know how Lana is going to survive this," Mom whispered. "I don't think I could go on if I lost either of the two of you."

Mom sat between us. I put my hand in hers and gave it a squeeze, and Stormy did the same on her side. Mom could be sharp-tongued at times, but she never meant any of it to be unkind.

"You'd have to lock me up in the loony bin if I lost one of my kids," Stormy whispered back. Stormy had five kids, and I knew what she said was true.

I didn't have any children, but I understood completely what they were saying. Losing somebody so young and so dear to you was unimaginable. If we lost any of my nieces and nephews, it would be devastating for me.

I looked up as Alex Stedman walked in the church. He was the last person I expected to see since he had fired Daphne.

I watched as he headed across the back of the room and stood behind the last pew at the end and looked toward the open casket. I wondered if he would go up and pay his respects to Daphne and her family. I also wondered what her family's reaction would be since they knew he had fired her. I leaned forward in my seat slightly and looked at Stormy, giving a slight nod of my head toward Alex. She turned to look and narrowed her eyes at him, watching him for a moment, then turned back to me and shrugged.

I sat back against the pew and wondered about this. As far as I knew, he hadn't had any interaction with Daphne after he had fired her, other than at the fall party. Or at least that's what he had implied when I spoke to him. His presence here at the funeral gave me pause and made me wonder exactly why he was here. I was suspicious. Maybe he was feeling guilty for something he had done. And maybe he was the reason Daphne was in that casket.

Just as the pastor stood and took the podium, I saw Jack Farrell walk in the door. He glanced in Alex's direction and frowned, hesitating. Then he headed in the opposite direction and took a seat. The people on that pew had to squeeze over to make room for him. I was also surprised at his presence since he and Daphne had broken up. But maybe he was grieving her death because of the time they spent together as a couple. Maybe he had regrets or wanted closure.

When my ex-husband eventually passed away from his brain tumor, would I feel the same way? Would I go to his funeral? I had been asking myself these questions for several weeks now, and I still didn't know the answers. Our marriage had ended terribly, and he had hurt me in ways I didn't think it was possible to be hurt. But there had been times that we were happy. We had had a beautiful, lavish wedding that he paid for and a wonderful honeymoon in Paris. Somewhere in my basement was a box that contained pictures from that trip. I had intended to dispose of them, but somehow never got around to doing it. My wedding book was also in that box. I wondered why I had hung onto them.

On the front pew, Bryan's shoulders shook as he broke down, and I felt a stab of pain in my chest. I could hardly stand the thought of what the family must be going through. At the end of the pew, next to Tim, Gina sat stoically. Did she feel guilty about the arguments she had had with Daphne? Did she feel regret for being unable to get along with her? It was a shame that they couldn't put their differences aside and at least have peace for the rest of the family's sake.

As I watched, I saw Gina look over her shoulder at the crowd. She gave a roll of her eyes and a shake of her head as if she couldn't believe all these people had shown up for Daphne's funeral. She turned back around and slouched down in the pew, looking for all the world like she was bored out of her mind. Her husband glanced in her direction and put a hand on her arm. She shook it off and looked up at the ceiling, shaking her head again, Anger rose up inside of me. She should at least have the decency to understand that her husband's family was hurting and give them some respect, if not sympathy. Once again I thought that maybe their arguing wasn't as superficial as she would have it seem.

When the service was over, we stood to walk past the casket and speak a word to the family. Stormy moved next to me. "I feel funny about Alex being here," she whispered.

I nodded. "I was thinking the same thing," I whispered back. "If what he said about letting her go from her job is true, then I can't imagine why he would be here. But maybe he really does feel terrible about having to fire her. Maybe he had some good memories of Daphne and just wanted to say goodbye to her."

She nodded and looked in Alex's direction. He was hanging back from the line of people that were headed down the aisle of the church. I wondered if he would go and speak to her family or take one last look at Daphne. Then I glanced over at Jack. Both of them seemed to be out of place here. I wondered if I would be out of place going to my ex-husband's funeral.

Mom looked back over her shoulder at us. "I don't know if I can speak to her parents. It's breaking my heart."

"We'll all go together, and it'll be okay," I said, reassuring her.

She nodded hesitantly. "Okay, as long as the two of you are with me, I can do this."

I reached forward and put a hand on her shoulder and gave it a squeeze. Mom was a softy at heart.

Chapter Sixteen

WHILE I WAS WORKING at the paper one afternoon, Gina Richards walked through the front door. Most of the staff was at lunch, and I was covering the front counter, helping out with subscription requests, advertisements, and anything else the public might need to come into the office for. Much of the work was done online, but Sparrow was a small town. Many people still preferred to do things the old-fashioned way by walking in and talking to someone face-to-face.

I got up from my desk and headed to the front counter to greet Gina. "Hi, Gina," I said, trying to sound chipper. "How are you today?" It had been a week since Daphne's funeral, and I hadn't seen anyone from the Richards family since that day.

She smiled back. "Things are going great! I think we're going to open the flower shop on the first of November. I know it's a little way off yet, but I wanted to take out an ad in the paper to announce the upcoming grand opening. I'm thinking I may put a little tease in the paper to get people excited."

"A tease? What do you mean?" I asked.

"Oh you know, I'm thinking about running an ad that says something like 'look what's coming to Sparrow soon,'" she said and giggled. "I want to stir up the public's interest with a little mystery, and by the time we get around to actually opening the shop, people will be champing at the bit to come in and see what we've got."

I nodded slowly. My mother had a wonderful flower shop, and I wasn't afraid for her or her business. At least, I was pretty sure I wasn't. But I'll admit that the more I thought about it, the more it bugged me that Gina was opening this shop.

"That sounds like fun," I said noncommittally. "Let me get you a form, and you can fill out what you want the ad to say." We had a form where the advertiser could choose the size of the ad and what they wanted it to say. I slid it across the desk to her.

She picked it up, looked it over, and then picked up a pen lying on the counter. "I want something big." She checked the box for a quarter-page ad. It surprised me. It was expensive to put an ad that size in the paper. Then she began filling out exactly what she wanted the ad to say.

"So, how are Tim and the family doing?" I asked as she filled out the form.

She continued writing without answering right away. Then she looked up at me and grinned. "They'll make it." She went back to filling out the form.

I was taken aback. "I'm sure losing a daughter and a sister has got to be a terribly traumatic experience."

She shrugged without looking at me. "I guess so," she said.

I gritted my teeth. I couldn't stand her attitude about Daphne's death. Sure, they had issues, but a lot of people have issues and can still manage to feel bad if someone dies.

"I feel terrible for Daphne's parents," I said. I probably should have left things alone, but I just couldn't. "Losing a daughter is terrible. Losing a sister is terrible too. Devastating."

She finished filling out the paper for the ad and slid it across to me. I glanced at it. It was very simple. Like she said, just a tease about a new business opening up. These would probably be very effective if she intended to do a lot of them prior to opening. That possibility disappointed me for some reason.

"Rainey, I know a lot of people feel that Daphne's death is a terrible thing. But I don't think there's any way I'm ever going to feel like that."

I looked at her and nodded slowly. "I guess some people have no heart where others are concerned."

She narrowed her eyes, and her jaw tensed visibly. "I don't care what you think about me, Rainey. But if you have any ideas that I had something to do with Daphne's death, you're insane. I don't hate anyone that much. But I sure don't feel sorry that she died."

"Fair enough. I guess no one can make you have feelings when there just aren't any available to have," I said, looking her in the eye. There was a little voice in my head telling me to shut up, but my mouth wasn't listening.

"If you want to take a look at someone—and I know that's what you're doing, by the way. It's not like anyone in Sparrow doesn't know that you're dating the detective on the case and that you're one of the nosiest people in town. You can take a look at Alex Stedman."

I felt my own jaw go tight now. There was so much I wanted to say, but I knew Cade would be angry if I completely let loose and said what I was thinking. "And why do you say that?"

She gave me a smirky little smile. "Because he didn't fire Daphne like he's been telling people. He sexually harassed her, and when she refused to give in to him, he threatened to fire her. But she turned the tables on him and blackmailed him, telling him she would expose him if he didn't pay her off." She tilted her head back and laughed. "Daphne told people she got fired so they would feel sorry for her, and everyone stupidly believed her."

I tried to keep the surprise off my face, but I'm pretty sure I failed at it. "And did he do it? Did he sexually harass her?" I knew what Jack had said, but I wasn't sure I believed it. Gina made the third person that brought this up, when you counted what Karen said.

"I have no idea if he actually sexually harassed her. It wouldn't surprise me one bit if she lied about it," she said, still with that smirky smile. "But Daphne said he paid her ten thousand dollars to keep her mouth shut."

"That's a lot of hush money if he didn't do anything wrong. How do you know he actually paid her the money?" I wasn't sure that I believed her. It was a lot of money for anyone to pay out to keep someone quiet if they were innocent.

"Oh he paid it all right," she said. "Daphne used it as a down payment on her new BMW. He didn't want it to get out about the possibility he had sexually harassed Daphne because his company was already struggling financially. And if Daphne started talking—and I know that she would have done that—it would have destroyed his company."

A picture of the new BMW we had seen parked at the lodge the night of the party flashed across my mind. What Gina was saying was breathtaking. I wouldn't have thought something like this of Alex, but when three people brought up similar stories, it was hard to say it couldn't have happened. And something inside me said it was true. "Well, that's interesting news." I wanted to keep things neutral. I didn't want Gina thinking she had gotten the better of me by knowing something this important about the case. And suddenly I realized why Daphne had so much trouble with Gina. Daphne had always had all the attention in the family. When Gina came along, she was arrogant and demanding of the attention that Daphne had always commanded. They were jealous of one another.

"So you see, Rainey," she said. "Just because someone acts like they're innocent doesn't mean they are. As far as I'm concerned, my money's on Alex Stedman as the killer. And if you had any smarts, you'd put your money on him too and let that detective know what I just told you."

She tossed a credit card on the front counter to pay for her ad. I had to force my hand to come out of the tightly gripped fist it had become, pick it up, and run it through the card reader to pay for the ad. "Well, Gina, it's certainly interesting. But I know the detective is looking into all of these things. And whoever that killer is," I said, looking her in the eye now. "I'm sure he'll figure it out soon, and they'll wish they had never done what they did. Spending the rest of one's life in jail isn't going to be much fun."

The smile slipped from her face as she glared at me. "Just you remember what I told you. Alex Stedman killed Daphne." She took the credit card back from me and stormed out of the newspaper office.

I watched her go, wishing I could keep that smirk off her face forever. Alex Stedman certainly had good reason to murder Daphne, even if he was innocent of sexual harassment. With Daphne threatening to sue him and his business already suffering, he might have felt trapped. Had she gotten the upper hand on him and forced him to pay her hush money?

Chapter Seventeen

I TURNED THE CORNER, my arms filled with plates of burgers, cold sandwiches, and a steak, when I almost ran right into Alex Stedman. I stopped on my heels, my eyes going to the plates in my arms, saying a silent prayer that I didn't spill anything.

"Oh, Rainey," Alex said, taking a step back. "I almost ran right into you. I'm sorry, I was just headed back to my table."

I looked up at him and frowned. The conversation I'd had with Gina Richards from two days earlier went through my mind. I thought I knew Alex, and now I wasn't so sure.

"That's okay. Things like that happen," I said brightly and went around him, heading to my table without another word. I hadn't seen him come in, but it had been busy and I hadn't had time to do anything other than attend to my tables.

"Here we are." I set the plates down in front of the hungry diners, hoping I had gotten the right plates in front of the right customers.

"This looks so good," the older woman said, looking over the Hawaiian burger I had set in front of her.

"Sam's serves the best burgers around," I promised her. "Can I get you all anything else?"

No one needed anything else, so I headed to my next table. I stopped in my tracks when I realized that Alex was sitting at one of my tables. One of the other girls must have shown him to the table. Sam's wasn't fancy enough to have a hostess, so sometimes people took whatever table was available, or one of us waitresses would seat them.

I pulled my order book out of my apron pocket and pasted a smile on my face. "Well, Alex, do you know what you want?"

He looked up from the menu in front of him. "I think I'm going to go with the clam chowder. I haven't had it in ages, and I know it's always great here."

"And to drink?" I didn't want to be rude, but I didn't want to make small talk either.

"Iced tea would be great."

I jotted down his order, nodded at him, and reached for the menu. "I'll be right back with that."

I turned and left before he could say anything else, my nerves suddenly on edge. I had gone over and over what Gina had said about him and had convinced myself that it must be true. Daphne had that shiny new BMW parked in front of the lodge on the night of the party. Where else would she have gotten the money? Her parents could have given it to her, but with her history of DUIs, I couldn't see them doing that. I stopped off at the soft drink fountain and made a glass of iced tea, then went into the kitchen and ladled up a bowl of clam chowder and got some crackers.

"Rainey, it seems like it's been forever since you made anything for us. I bet you still need us to try out the recipes for that new cookbook and I hope that job at the newspaper isn't keeping you too occupied," Sam said from his place next to the grill. He gave me a grin.

"I seem to remember a cinnamon crumb cake the other day," I pointed out.

"That seems like it was a while ago," he said, sounding disappointed.

"Oh, Sam, I guess I've been busier than usual. I've had lamb chops on my mind. How about you buy the meat, and I'll bring in the rest of the ingredients and cook them here? Maybe you can make them a lunch special?"

"That sounds great," he said. "And now that the holidays are almost here, we're going to get to taste some wonderful holiday treats, aren't we?"

"I'm sure we will," I answered. I headed back out to Alex's table, picked up the glass of iced tea on the way, and brought the clam chowder and crackers to him. Thankfully he had ordered something easy, so I didn't have to hang around his table.

"I saw you at Daphne's funeral," he said as I set the clam chowder in front of him.

I set the tea down. "I saw you too. I was a little surprised at that if you want to know the truth." It was out of my mouth before I thought it through.

He looked at me, eyebrows raised. "Surprised? Daphne worked for me for three years. I felt bad about what happened to her, and I wanted to pay my respects."

I folded my arms across my chest, feeling defensive. "Did you really?"

He looked at me for a moment before answering. "I did. Why? Why do you say it like that?"

I shrugged. "Can I ask you a personal question?" I hated to do this at the diner, but he was here and my attitude toward him was showing anyway.

His mouth made a straight line. "Sure, go ahead and ask."

"Was Daphne going to sue you for sexual harassment?" It was a blunt question, but I thought I might as well give it to him straight.

His eyes went big, his mouth forming a hard line. "She threatened me with a lawsuit, but I can tell you with all honesty that I never laid a hand on her."

"Sexual harassment isn't just about laying a hand on someone," I said. "There are a lot of other things that fall under the category of sexual harassment."

He shook his head. "Rainey, I don't know what you've heard, but it's not true. I would never do something like that. Not to Daphne, not to anybody. Who told you this?"

I shrugged. "I don't know that it makes any difference. But I heard that you settled out of court because you were afraid of the attention it would draw to your business and that your business was already suffering financially."

He looked at a spot on the table in front of him and then looked back up at me. "You want to know the truth? I'll tell you the truth. Daphne lied. Her drinking had gotten so bad she was coming in to work under the influence and she would come on to me. But I told her I wasn't interested. I mean, what interest would I have in somebody who was drunk all the time? It made her mad, and she threatened me with a sexual harassment lawsuit to get back at me."

I considered this. Daphne was drunk a lot, and it wouldn't surprise me if she went to work drunk. But had she come on to him? I didn't think anybody was going to know the answer to that except him since Daphne was gone. "But why pay her off like that? It makes you look guilty. And ten thousand dollars? That's an awful lot of money if you were innocent. You did pay her ten thousand dollars, didn't you?"

He nodded his head. "It is a lot of money. And I refused to do it at first. But you know about the Richards family. You know how much money they have. She threatened to get the best lawyer money could afford and drag my name through the mud. I felt like I had no choice, and I thought it would be cheaper to just pay the money rather than try to defend myself in the public eye." He narrowed his eyes and looked me up and down, considering me. It made me uncomfortable. Had I just made a killer angry?

"Do you really think that would have happened? I mean, if it did go public, do you really think it would have hurt your business so much that you couldn't have recovered from it?" I asked him. "It seems to me that having people find out you paid hush money would hurt your business a lot more than a sexual harassment lawsuit."

His mouth formed a hard line, and he gritted his teeth for a moment before answering. "It was more than just my business. It was my reputation. I don't want to go through life with the stigma of sexual predator hanging over my head. Would you? I mean come on, I'm still young and I have other aspirations. I might run for public office further down the road."

I took this in. Alex had always been active in speech and drama in school, and it wouldn't surprise me a bit if he decided to go into politics at some point in time. And it would have made things difficult with a sexual harassment lawsuit in his past. I still didn't know if he was telling me the truth or if Gina was. Daphne could have lied to everyone about the sexual harassment. I relaxed my stance. "Well then, I'm sorry to hear that Daphne would do something like that to you." It seemed like staying neutral for now was the best move.

"You don't know the half of what that woman was capable of. If you want to know who I think killed her, I think it was Jack Farrell or maybe even the queen bee herself, Gina Richards." He smirked when he said the last part.

"Why? Why do you say it like that?"

"Why do you think Daphne and Jack broke up?" he asked, leaning back in his seat. "It was because Gina and Jack were having an affair." He grinned at me, allowing me to take this in.

I took a deep breath. As much as I hated to admit it, it was a possibility. Maybe that was why Gina and Daphne hated each other as much as they did. "Do you know this for a fact?"

He nodded. "The day Daphne found out about it, she came to work drunk. I couldn't believe she had driven all the way over to Boise in that state. She sat at her desk crying and sobbing about Jack cheating on her with Gina and she was going to let her brother Tim know about it, but she never did. Apparently, Gina had something on her."

"And what was that?"

He shrugged. "She wouldn't say, but a few days later when I told her she needed to tell her brother, she freaked out. She said there was no way she could do that to him. She started to say something about Gina knowing something and then she caught herself and said her reason for not telling him was that she didn't want to hurt her brother."

I sighed. Things were getting more complicated by the minute. The more I asked around, the more one thing led to another. But it seemed that everything always led back to Gina. If what Alex said was true, and he wasn't the one who killed Daphne, then Gina had the most reason to do it.

Chapter Eighteen

BY THE TIME I GOT DONE working at Sam's for the afternoon, I was exhausted. The weather had turned cold with the wind blowing and the sky overcast and threatening rain. I decided I needed a nice hot coffee to help me regain my energy.

I walked into the British Tea and Coffee Company and spotted Cade at a table with Agatha. I headed to him and leaned over and gave him a quick kiss, then sat down. "Hi, Agatha," I said to her. "My feet are aching."

"Hello yourself, lovely," she said. "Can I get you a coffee?"

"A pumpkin spice latte would be wonderful, but you don't need to get up and get it. Let me put my purse down and rest my feet for a minute and then I'll go and get one from the front."

"Nonsense," she said, getting to her feet. "I'll get you a nice hot coffee, and you relax here with your lovely man."

Cade grinned at her words and took a sip of his coffee. "So, how is my little detective's assistant doing today?"

I looked at him, one eyebrow raised. "So now I'm a detective's assistant?"

"You are if you've got any new information for me," he said with a grin.

"Just that Daphne led a rather wild life. Her drinking really was out of control and she ran around a lot, but I guess that isn't new. I also learned that she threatened to bring a sexual harassment lawsuit against her former employer, Alex Stedman. He, of course, denies the wrongdoing, but not the threat."

He took this in. "Do you believe him?"

I shrugged. "I really thought he was a nice guy in school, but I do have my doubts now. Of course, Gina Richards is the one who told me about it, to begin with, and Alex says that she and Daphne's boyfriend Jack Farrell had an affair. Honestly, it wouldn't surprise me if everybody was lying."

He nodded. "It seems that in the case of murder, people are going to do that. You have no idea the stories I've heard over the years."

"I bet," I said. "I don't know how you do it. Wouldn't you rather be a veterinarian? At least animals wouldn't lie to you about what was wrong with them."

"No, but they bite and I'm completely against being bitten," he said and took another sip of his coffee.

"There is that," I said. "So what do you know that's new?"

"We can't find anything else with any traces of the poison from the items we gathered from the party. Of course, something could have been missed. But nobody else got sick so we're assuming the poison was just in this one cup that only Daphne drank from."

"I do remember seeing Daphne carrying around a Styrofoam cup," I said. "So that means the killer gave her the cup. She probably wouldn't have taken it from them unless she knew them well."

"I have somebody I want you to speak to," he said and looked over his shoulder. "Daphne's brother Mark. When I spoke to him he seemed evasive."

"Mark? I wondered about him losing that job to Daphne," I said thoughtfully. "But I've talked to him a couple of times, and he does appear to be grieving his sister."

He nodded. "Some people are good actors. And it may have been just general nervousness and not evasiveness when I spoke to him. Some people get that way when talking to the police."

Agatha returned with a large latte and set it in front of me. "Thank you, Agatha, you're a saint." I picked it up, inhaled the scent of wonderful pumpkin-flavored coffee, and then took a deep drink.

Agatha chuckled. "I don't know if I've ever been called a saint before," she said and laughed again. "But I'll take it. Thank you."

"Well, people should be calling you a saint more often," I said.

"I was trying to pry information out of your man about Daphne's murder, but he sure is tight-lipped," she explained to me. "Are you going to be as tight-lipped as he is? Or are you going to spill what you know?"

I glanced at Cade, who just grinned and shrugged. "I guess it all depends on what you want to know," I said.

"Well, darling, I want to know if we know who killed her? Whoever it is needs to be hung high. Is hanging a thing anymore?"

Cade chuckled. "No, hanging isn't a thing anymore."

"Poor Daphne," I said and took another sip of my coffee. "What a terrible thing to have happened. Maybe we should see if the state will reinstate hanging once the killer is caught?"

"Do you want to know something?" Agatha asked, leaning in and speaking quietly. "I saw Daphne with another man when she was supposed to be dating Jack Farrell. I never understood it. Jack is such a handsome man, and he always seems so nice. But I didn't want to upset anyone, so I never said anything to him."

"Do you know who she was with? Had you seen him before?" I asked.

She shook her head. "He looked vaguely familiar, but I don't know who he was. My friend and I were in a restaurant in Boise when I saw them. As the evening wore on, Daphne had a bit too much to drink, and when they left, she was staggering and laughing loudly. It seemed that everyone in the restaurant was staring."

I looked at Cade, who was considering this. "It seems Daphne had a habit of running around with different men."

"Makes you sad for what this world is coming to when people behave that way," Agatha said thoughtfully. "I hate to sound like an old woman, but back in my day, people didn't run around like that." She laughed. "I guess that does make me sound like an old woman, doesn't it? Just a judgmental old thing."

"I think everyone wishes for simpler times now and then," I said and put my hand over hers. Agatha was a dear friend, and I didn't blame her for what she was thinking.

"The other thing I heard was that Daphne and her brother Mark fought a lot," Agatha said without looking at either of us.

"I hate to say terrible things about that family because they've always been so good to me and everyone I know."

"What do you know about it?" I asked. "Anything specific?" I glanced at Cade again.

Agatha kept her eyes on her hands in front of her. "It's silly, really. But Mark had a tantrum one day at the lodge, saying that his parents favored Daphne over him. It would've been laughable if he had been a youngster at the time, but it was last year when it happened, and he was far too old to behave that way. I tell you, Rainey, it was like he was a spoiled nine-year-old." On the last part she looked up at me, her eyebrows furrowed.

"That's odd." Cade looked only mildly interested in the conversation, and I considered kicking him under the table to make sure he was paying attention to what Agatha was saying.

"I do know that the Richardses are good people," Agatha said. "And I hope no one's going to blame anything on anyone in that family." She looked pointedly at Cade.

"My job is to find the killer, regardless of who it is," Cade spoke up. "Any information is helpful, and we'll keep it in the strictest confidence." He looked at me.

Agatha nodded. "Of course, Detective. Now then, can I get you a refill on your pumpkin spice latte?" she asked him.

He looked embarrassed for a moment, then handed her his cup. "Thank you, Agatha."

"So, are you into silly froufrou drinks now?" I asked him. Cade usually drank his coffee plain or with just a little sugar and cream.

"Don't ever call pumpkin spice latte a silly froufrou drink," he said in a mock-stern tone.

I laughed. "All right then. Pumpkin spice lattes. Coffee of men."

He tried to look at me with a straight face but ended up grinning. "We need to go out again soon. Very soon."

"You don't have to ask me twice," I said softly. "Whenever you can get a little time away from this case, I'm ready."

"How about Friday night? Wherever you want to go."

"Friday is my very favorite night of the whole week," I said. "I'll be ready."

We sat and gazed at one another, waiting for Agatha to come back with his refill. I could do this for hours without getting tired of it.

Chapter Nineteen

"DO YOU KNOW WHAT I saw today?" My mother asked.

"Not exactly, but I might be able to guess," I said into the phone. I knew Gina's ad for her new flower shop had run in the evening paper the day before. I was pretty sure that's what Mom was talking about, but I didn't want to volunteer it if she hadn't seen it yet.

"An ad in your newspaper advertising a new business being opened up," she said, breathing heavily into the phone.

My eyes went to George Cooper at the desk across from mine. I was at the newspaper trying to write an article on Thanksgiving traditions. "I have never owned this newspaper," I said into the phone and turned away from George.

"Well, when is the new flower shop supposed to open up? I bet you know that, don't you?" Her tone was accusatory, and I wasn't sure why.

"Mom, I do know when it's going to open, but it's not like I had anything to do with it. It's going to open the first of November," I whispered into the phone. I knew she was upset about it, but I wasn't sure it was my place to fill her in.

"Just as I suspected. Gina Richards is trying to horn in on my business for the holidays," she said.

"Mom, you knew at some point that someone would open up another flower shop, didn't you? You have nothing to worry about. People have been coming to you for years. Even when Celia Markson's shop was still around, people came to you because they know that you offer a quality product and you do beautiful work," I assured her. It was the truth. My mother could take a handful of weeds and artfully arrange them in a glass vase and make them beautiful.

She sighed. "It seems like my own daughter would have let me know when a competitive business was going to open up."

"Mom, I'm sorry. I thought you were going to speak to Gina anyway, and I thought she would bring it up to you. And Mom, I've got to go. I've got an article that I've got to get done before my deadline."

"Okay, fine," she said. "You go on and write your article for that traitor newspaper. But you remember who your real friends are."

I sighed. "I love you, Mom," I said and hung up the phone. Mom had a flair for the dramatic.

When I turned around in my seat, George was looking at me. I smiled and shrugged.

"So has that detective you're dating found that girl's killer yet?" he asked casually. George looked to be in his late forties with curly blond hair and a thick mustache. He had mostly kept to himself since I had begun working here, with just a grunt of hello now and then. I didn't know much about him.

"Not yet, but I'm sure the police will get it sorted out any day now."

He nodded. "You know, her boyfriend Jack Farrell tried to sell me some pictures."

I stared at him. "What do you mean 'pictures'? What kind of pictures?"

"Compromising pictures. He owns a photography business, you know, and I guess she let him take some pictures."

My heart started pounding in my chest. How does a boyfriend take compromising pictures of his girlfriend and then offer to sell them to a reporter? "Why would he do something like that?"

"He wanted to embarrass the Richardses. He thought he could get the girl back by blackmailing her with the pictures, but when she laughed at him, he came to me, hoping I would buy them from him."

"And did you see the pictures?" I asked him.

He nodded. "I saw them. Sure, they were kind of compromising, but I've seen worse. But it's not like I was going to put something like that in the newspaper. The guy had to be out of his mind."

It didn't make sense. "Right. I mean, under what circumstances would he think you would put them in the local paper?"

He nodded. "The younger brother, Mark, wanted to run for mayor. Jack thought he could embarrass the entire family if she refused to go out with him again."

"So if she agreed to go out with him, he wouldn't sell you the pictures?"

He nodded. "That's exactly it. He said he had other pictures even more compromising, and he was just showing me a couple to whet my appetite." He chuckled. "I thought the guy was crazy."

I felt sick to my stomach. Was Jack really that depraved to think that he could blackmail Daphne into getting back together with him? What kind of relationship would that be? And what kind of person would want a relationship like that? It made me wonder if that kind of person would kill another person when he didn't get what he wanted. I thought the answer to that question was yes.

"It does sound crazy," I agreed with him.

"You know what else? I heard a rumor around town that Alex Stedman had sexually harassed her."

"That rumor does seem to be going around town," I agreed. I wasn't going to give him any more information than he already knew.

"I also heard Alex Stedman paid her ten grand to keep her from taking him to court over it." He sat back in his chair and twirled a pencil between his fingers.

"Who did you hear that from?" I asked him. Not that it mattered. Too many people already knew about it.

He chuckled again. "Gina Richards. She didn't keep it a secret. That family has issues."

Gina needed to learn to keep her mouth shut. Was she so angry and bitter toward Daphne that she ran her mouth all over town? It appeared that was the case and it irritated me.

"You know, Daphne's parents, Lana and Bryan, are really nice people. I've known them most of my life. I just feel really had that their daughter died, and that their daughter-in-law is spreading rumors around town," I said. I felt like I had to stick up for them in their time of trouble.

"I agree with you on that. I don't think you'd ever meet nicer people than Bryan and Lana. But here's the thing," he said, leaning forward over the desk. "Alex Stedman never had the money to pay her off. I did an article on his new business when he first opened it, and he told me he was running it on a shoestring. He said he barely had the starting capital for just the bare bones operations."

"What do you mean he didn't have the money? Going into any business is expensive," I said. "He had to have money." I wondered if Alex had told him the truth, or had his business turned itself around in the time that he had it open?

"You bet it costs a lot of money," he said. "But we hung out for a while and talked, and he told me he had to get a loan for startup capital and the payments were eating him alive. He worried he wouldn't be in business long."

"That's been a few years ago. Don't you think he's made enough money now so that he's better off financially?"

He smiled. "That's the hope of most businesses. That once they get going, they'll bring in enough capital to make it, but I saw where he filed for personal bankruptcy back in June."

I was stunned. If Alex filed for bankruptcy back in June, how could he have paid Daphne the ten thousand dollars? Or was the reason he had to file for bankruptcy because he had paid Daphne the money? Things weren't adding up.

"Bankruptcies are public, aren't they?" I asked him.

He nodded. "The newspaper holds an account where we can view that information."

Gina had said that Daphne had put the money down on a new BMW. I had seen the BMW parked at the lodge, and if Daphne was unemployed, how did she pay for the car?

"I'm sure Cade will get to the bottom of this thing soon," I said slowly. I smiled at him to cover for the fact that my head was spinning with what he had told me.

"I'm sure he will. But you might put a bug in his ear about these things. In my opinion, either Alex Stedman or Jack Farrell could have killed Daphne, and I'd hate to see them get away with murder."

"No one's going to get away with murder," I assured him. "And I agree, if these things are true, it does make you wonder if either Jack or Alex could have been responsible for Daphne's murder."

I turned back to my computer and stared at the article I had begun earlier. My mind turned with this new information, and I found myself unable to concentrate on the article. What had Daphne gotten herself into? It made me sick to think of the twisted web that surrounded her life. I shook off the thoughts and tried to focus on the article I was writing. Thanksgiving would be here before we knew it, and I was getting excited just thinking about it. But Daphne's murder weighed heavily on my mind. It felt like we needed one more piece of the puzzle to get this thing sorted out and put a killer behind bars.

Chapter Twenty

I STOOD IN FRONT OF the collage of pictures that Jack Farrell had taken of Daphne. They were arranged on a small table and displayed in carved wood frames. The more I looked at them, the more I thought it was almost a shrine to Daphne. It made me wonder how long this little collection had been on display in Jack's shop. It hadn't been long after Daphne died that I had stopped in to speak to him the first time, and I had only seen the photos on the wall. Had he set up the arrangement after killing Daphne? I shook myself. I was jumping to conclusions, but the fact that he had tried to get money for pictures of Daphne infuriated me.

Jack was busy with a customer, coming out of his studio with a young mother and her toddler daughter in tow. When he saw me, he looked surprised for a moment, then he smiled and nodded while continuing to speak to the mother. I wondered if she knew that the man taking pictures of her daughter might be a murderer.

I looked around the shop and saw a new photo that I was sure hadn't been there when I was in last. Daphne was leaning against a tree, hands in her jean pockets and a smile on her face.

Was I imagining things? Or did I just not remember seeing this picture the last time I was here?

Jack finished up his business with the woman and she left the shop.

"Hello, Rainey. How are you today?" he asked, extending a hand to me.

I turned around and smiled, extending my own hand to shake his. "I'm great," I said. "How are you today, Jack?"

"I'm doing great," he said with a smile. Jack was handsome with his ginger hair and blue eyes. "Are you ready to take that author photo? I was wondering when you'd be back in."

"I still need to do that, don't I?" I said, and then I looked at that picture on the wall. "Tell me, Jack, was this picture here when I came in a couple of weeks ago?"

He looked at it and then turned back to me. "No, I found it on a roll of film I developed and thought how nice Daphne looked in it. I decided to blow it up and frame it and put it on my wall to remember her by."

"Film? Do many photographers use film these days?" Cade had told me that Jack had a fondness for film and creating sepia-tone photographs, but I wanted to see what he had to say about it.

He chuckled. "Not many, but some of us still do. I have a fondness for actual film. As a matter fact, I probably took the last photography class in high school that was ever offered in the country." He chuckled. "I'm joking, of course. But it seems like it was; it's been a few years since I was in high school. I learned to develop my own film old-school. I just enjoy the process so much."

"Really? I can see where that would almost be a lost art form, what with all the computer programs that can create different effects. It makes it so easy to edit photos these days, doesn't it?"

He nodded. "Yes, it sure does make it easy. But I still enjoy using real film from time to time. Daphne and I went out near the river, and I took probably fifty or sixty pictures of her that day. I wish I'd kept them all, but I had tossed a lot of them when they didn't turn out as well as I had hoped. Then I found a roll that I hadn't completely taken all the pictures on and this one was on it."

I nodded. "Is it hard to get the equipment and chemicals that you need to develop film?"

"You can get it on the internet. Lots of people think it's time to do away with darkrooms and just go completely digital, but I love the medium. It's so hands on."

"I didn't realize you could still buy the film and chemicals."

He nodded. "It's not hard to find it," he said. "Are you interested in having some pictures done with film?"

I thought about this. It would be fun to take up photography, and I could see the appeal of developing your own film, especially making the sepia-tone photos.

"You know what I'm really interested in?" I asked him.

He looked at me, sensing something in my tone. "No, Rainey, what's that?"

"What I'm wondering is why you tried to sell photos of Daphne to George Cooper at the newspaper."

His mouth formed a hard line, and his hands curled up into balls. "Who told you that?"

"I have a part-time job down at the newspaper. Let's just say it came up in conversation," I said. Too late I realized that he was blocking the door. I needed to work on when I sprang bad news on people. Especially when those people were a lot bigger than I was.

"I may have done something like that, but I deeply regret my actions. Daphne didn't deserve for me to do something like that to her. I guess jealousy got the better of me and I was angry. She cheated on me and then broke up with me, blaming everything that was bad in our relationship on me. I hate when people don't take responsibility for their actions," he said, relaxing a little.

I nodded. "I guess I can see where that would make a person angry, but I can't see where that would make a person try to sell compromising pictures of their ex-girlfriend to the newspaper."

He considered me for a moment. "Wait a minute. Didn't you tell me that you were dating the detective looking into Daphne's murder?"

"I might have," I said, trying to remember back if I had told him that or not.

"Are you asking me this because you think I murdered Daphne?" He looked at me, tilting his head to the side.

"I don't know, Jack, did you murder Daphne?" I asked, folding my arms in front of my chest. Cade hated when I asked people if they had committed murder, but since we were on the subject, I thought I might as well.

He shook his head, his eyes going wide. "No! I did not kill Daphne. I would never ever kill her or anyone else. Does that detective think that I killed her?" I could see the panic in his eyes, and it surprised me. He had gone from seeming almost sinister to looking like a kid got that had just been called up to the principal's office.

"Cade doesn't let me in on everything he knows about a case," I said calmly. "It wouldn't be right, now would it? But when I hear from somebody that you were trying to sell compromising pictures of Daphne, it does cause me some concern. Just as a friend of the victim's family, you understand."

He shook his head again. "I promise you, I would never harm Daphne. Like I said, I was angry. I made a stupid decision, but I would never hurt her in any way. And besides, if you want to look at somebody who may have hurt Daphne, why don't you look at her brother Mark?"

"Why would I do that?" I asked him.

"Because when Daphne told him I had tried to sell the pictures to George, he came to me and said he wanted in on the action."

It was my turn to be surprised. "Why on earth would he want to do that? I thought he wanted to run for mayor of Sparrow and that's why you wanted to sell the pictures."

"He told me running for mayor was just a whim and that he had no intention of doing it. But he thought that Daphne would be embarrassed enough knowing that there were pictures of her out there floating around that she would pay to keep them from coming to light."

I shook my head slowly. "I don't believe a word you're saying. It doesn't make sense that he would try to get money out of his sister. That family is reasonably well off, and as far as I can tell, Mark has never had a reason to want for money."

He shrugged. "For some people, enough money is never enough. All I know is he wanted to threaten his sister with the possibility of those pictures being put out on the internet. He didn't care about the local newspaper, and I have to admit that was a stupid move anyway. But he wanted her to know that if she didn't give him the money, then the whole world was going to see those pictures."

"He didn't want to see the pictures, did he?" I had to ask.

He chuckled. "No. He had no interest in seeing them. He didn't even care if they actually existed as long as his sister thought they did. And as a side note, there wasn't anything more provocative than the ones I showed George. I just told him that there were."

"Why did she think they existed?" I asked.

"She drank a lot. She couldn't remember."

I sighed. The games people played. "And how much was Mark asking for?"

"A cool ten grand."

My stomach churned. Why did that figure keep coming up? I was having a hard time believing that her brother would want to humiliate her that way. "I think you're full of it."

"You're entitled to believe what you want. I destroyed the pictures. I decided I didn't really want anyone to see them."

"Why would I believe that?"

"I guess you don't have to believe that. But I felt terrible about the way things were going, and I decided I needed to change the way I was living. I gave up drinking, and I destroyed those pictures. After a while, I decided I was glad Daphne was out of my life, She was too much drama, and she was leading me down a really destructive path."

"Next thing you'll be saying is that you started going to church," I said snidely.

He grinned. "I've gone a couple of times. I told you, I didn't like the way I was living. When I was with Daphne, I was drinking all the time and it was destroying my life. I've got more to live for than booze," he said and then became somber. "I wish Daphne had wanted the same thing for herself."

I didn't know if Jack was telling me the truth or not. Part of it seemed far-fetched, and yet there was a ring of truth to all of it. But mostly I wished, just like he did, that Daphne had decided she wanted something better for her life, too.

Chapter Twenty-One

"ARE YOU DISAPPOINTED?"

I shrugged. "No," I said quietly as I ran a finger along the fork on the table in front of me.

"I'm sorry," Cade said. "I really do want to take you out someplace nice. You know work has been getting in the way lately."

I nodded and looked up at him. "I don't mind really. As long as I get to spend the evening with you, I'm not going to complain." We were sitting at the local pizza place waiting for our order to be brought to our table. Cade had promised me a nice evening out, but he had been detained at work. It was nearly 8 p.m. by the time he got free. He offered to take me out to a nicer restaurant anyway because there were restaurants in Boise that would be open late, but I knew he was tired. He needed a break, so I suggested pizza.

He reached a hand across the table and put it on mine, giving my hand a squeeze. "I sure am glad that you're as understanding as you are."

I grinned at him. "Of course I'm understanding because I know you're going to make it all up to me sometime soon."

He chuckled, "You know I will."

"So, should I even bother asking? Anything new?"

He shook his head. "Nope. Poor Daphne is still as dead as can be, your hot cider punch facilitated that murder, and we still have a few suspicious people, but no one willing to cop to the act."

"I wish you would quit pointing out that my cider helped kill Daphne," I muttered, narrowing my eyes at him.

He shrugged. "I cannot tell a lie, ma'am. You make a killer hot cider."

I narrowed my eyes at him again and snorted. If he weren't as cute as he was, I'd give him a piece of my mind. "I had some interesting conversations today."

"Do tell," he said, raising one eyebrow and taking a sip of his iced tea.

"George Cooper is a reporter for the newspaper, and we had a conversation about Daphne's death. He said Jack tried to sell him compromising photos of Daphne. He wanted to blackmail Daphne with them."

He looked at me, both eyebrows raised now. "Really? That's not a very nice way for a boyfriend to behave, ex or not."

"Right?" I said, leaning back in my seat. "I asked him about it, and he claimed he did it out of anger and regretted his actions. He said he never would have actually done it and that he had lied to George about how compromising the pictures were. But even more interesting, he said that Daphne's brother Mark wanted in on the action."

Cade looked at me open-mouthed. "Wait, you confronted Jack about him blackmailing Daphne? And then her brother wanted in on the action?"

I nodded. "I couldn't help myself. I had to go and speak to Jack about it. It infuriated me that he would do such a thing to her, and then he told me about Mark."

"Well I can appreciate that you went all girl power and everything and wanted to defend Daphne's honor, but you're not supposed to be accusing people of anything. You're supposed to be letting me know if you find something interesting."

"Well, Cade, I did find something interesting. He tried to blackmail her." I gave him a smirk and took a sip of my iced tea.

"You know I don't like when you do things like that," he said and picked up his own glass of tea and took another sip. "And explain Mark wanting in on the action. What is the so-called action?"

"The blackmail money." I don't know why he didn't understand that was what I was talking about.

He nodded slowly. "That is a bizarre development."

"That's exactly what I thought."

"What about the possibility that Jack is lying about it? Did you think about that?"

I gasped. "Of course I thought about that. I mean look, there is no reason for Jack or anybody else to be telling us the truth, is there? Especially if they murdered Daphne."

"Please tell me you didn't confront Mark about it," he said.

I shook my head. "I have been behaving myself on that one. I would hate to accuse anyone that just lost a family member to murder. And besides that, Mark said he and his siblings were very close to one another."

"Between you and me, I'm going to interview Alex Stedman again. That whole mess with a sexual harassment lawsuit and blackmail he was reportedly involved in doesn't sit right with me. I have my suspicions about him. And I'll add one more round with Jack Farrell and Mark Richards."

"I think you're exactly right about that," I said. "But I also have my eye on Gina. She's so bitter about everything. I think she makes Alex look like a happy, well-adjusted individual if you want to know the truth."

He chuckled. "I guess I have to agree with you on that. She's another person I need to speak with again."

I nodded. "So tell me, Cade, when are you not going to work so many hours?"

"When people quit murdering other people," he said. The waitress brought our pizza and set it down on the table in front of us. Half Hawaiian for me and a meat extravaganza for him. "This smells good."

"Seriously though, we should take a trip somewhere. Just the two of us," I said hopefully. I had never dated someone that made me so comfortable, and all I wanted was to spend more time with him.

"We could take a trip out to the river," he teased. He used the pizza server to put a piece of the meat extravaganza on his plate while I use the one on my side to get a piece of Hawaiian pizza onto my plate.

"Ha ha," I said. "The river is beautiful, and don't get me wrong, I do love it there. But it's getting too cold, and I'm not that big on camping anyway. I like indoor plumbing and electricity. Maybe we could go away someplace romantic."

"We can do that," he said. "You say the word, and if somebody hasn't been murdered anytime close to the time that you can get off work, we will go."

I chuckled. "You're making things difficult, are you?"

"It's not me that's out running around murdering people," he pointed out.

We looked up as Mark and Gina Richards walked into the restaurant. Cade and I watched as they headed to a corner table and sat down. We looked at each other and then turned back to look at them.

"Well, that's interesting," I whispered as we continued watching them. The waitress handed them menus, and when she left, they leaned forward and began whispering.

"Interesting isn't the word for it," Cade agreed. "I wonder where her husband is?"

"I wonder where his brother is?" I added.

We sat back and watched them awhile. They seemed oblivious to anyone around them. I wondered if Tim knew they were here together. If he didn't, they didn't seem to mind that people saw them together.

"Maybe they're just discussing the new business that Gina is opening," he said.

"They could be," I said, keeping an eye on them. "And I suppose if they were doing anything nefarious, they would be worried about people spotting them out together. Makes me wonder about the rumors of Gina's supposed affairs."

Cade turned back to me. "You would think so, wouldn't you?"

I nodded and took a bite of my pizza, considering this. Gina seemed to cause nothing but trouble in that family, but the two of them appeared to be enjoying one another's company now.

"How does your mother feel about that new flower shop she's opening?" Cade asked me.

I shrugged. "She hasn't come out and said it, but I think it really bothers her. And I think it probably bothers her more that no one mentioned it to her. Not that they had an obligation to do so, of course."

He nodded. "I don't think your mother has anything to worry about. People like your mom. They're kind of drawn to her, you know?" he said.

I knew he was telling the truth about that. Mom had lived here all her life, and she knew just about everyone in town. Still, I had to wonder about Gina and Mark having dinner together like they were. It made me suspicious.

Chapter Twenty-Two

I HAD A LOT TO THINK about over the next few days. While Cade was going to try to get more information from Mark, I wanted to see if I could find out anything else.

"Rainey, these lamb chops are the best I've ever eaten," Agatha said from her booth in the corner of the diner.

I smiled and slid into the seat across from her. It was after 1:30 in the afternoon, and the lunch crowd had thinned considerably. "Thanks, Agatha," I said. "I used quite a lot of garlic and some rosemary to bring out the flavor of the meat." I loved lamb chops but rarely made them. Lamb was more of a spring dish, but it could be bought year-round at the local grocery store.

"You've certainly outdone yourself this time," she said, dabbing at her mouth with her napkin. "It makes me wish I served savory dishes at the coffee shop." She giggled and laid her napkin down.

"Well that's something to think about," I agreed with a chuckle. "You could always put some on the menu for lunch and see how that goes."

She chuckled. "Now wouldn't that be something? Sam would be so mad at you if he knew you were trying to talk me into serving lunch at the coffee shop. But I suppose I could steal away his star employee, couldn't I?"

"You might be able to do that," I teased. "But Sam would never forgive me."

"I wouldn't blame him one bit. So how is Daphne's murder case going? Any news on the killer?" She whispered the last part, looking around to see if anyone was listening in.

I tried to be careful about disclosing exactly what I knew about the cases that Cade was working on. I didn't want to let anything slip that he might need to be kept quiet. "Oh you know how it is, Cade has been working night and day to get this thing solved. I bet he'll come up with something any day now. We can't have a killer running around the streets of Sparrow."

She nodded. "No, we need the killer caught right away."

The diner was nearly empty, so I took a seat across from her, keeping an eye out for new customers coming through the door. "I'm so glad the weather has turned cooler. I love the fall, with all the turning leaves."

"I do too," she said and took a sip of her hot tea. "I can't say I'm looking forward to the snow; my arthritis aches something awful when it gets really cold."

"I'm sorry to hear that," I said. "Maybe this winter won't be a severe one."

"You know, Rainey," Agatha said, glancing over her shoulder. None of the other customers were seated near her booth, and she turned back to me. "I have a funny feeling about Jack Farrell. I always felt like Daphne shouldn't be with him."

"Why do you say that?"

"I don't know, it's just a feeling I got. It seemed like he was very possessive of her. And he was always taking pictures of her. Even when they came into the coffee shop, it seemed like she couldn't sit still for a minute without him pulling out a camera or his phone and taking pictures of her."

"Even when they were just stopping in to get coffee?"

She nodded somberly. "It was odd. I mean in this day and age you get used to seeing people taking selfies or pictures of one another, but there is a limit to that, you know?"

I nodded. "It does get ridiculous with some people."

"Maybe I'm just being old-fashioned. It seems like it wasn't that long ago that people didn't behave that way," she said with a chuckle.

"It's interesting that he's really into using film. I've always had a bit of an interest in photography, but I've never followed through on learning to take pictures well."

She nodded. "Her brother Mark has an interest in it as well."

"Oh? I didn't know that."

She nodded. "He worked for Jack for a couple of months last year," she said. "I don't know why he stopped working there. I never asked him about it."

Now I was interested. "I had no idea he worked for Jack."

She nodded. "He came into the coffee shop one day with his hand bandaged. It didn't look like a bandage a doctor or hospital would put on, so I thought he must've hurt himself at the lodge somehow. I asked him what happened, and he said he got a burn from some chemicals used to develop photos."

"That's interesting. I suppose he must have spilled it on himself?"

She nodded. "He said he was being clumsy when helping Jack to develop some film. Apparently, Jack was out of the shop for a bit, and I guess Mark decided to go ahead and work on developing the film they had taken the day before."

I took this in. Jack's name kept popping up. "When I spoke to Mark, he seemed appropriately grieved about the loss of his sister."

"I don't doubt that," she said. "He's always said that they were close. But, Daphne never really spoke about her brother when I saw her."

"What do you mean?"

She shrugged. "I don't know. I would bring up his name in conversation occasionally, and she would just ignore it and change the subject. But you know how Daphne was. I don't mean to speak ill of the dead, but she was a bit self-absorbed. She was young of course, and sometimes young people are that way."

I nodded. "She was kind of different, wasn't she? I mean, different from her parents."

"That's exactly what I was thinking," Agatha said. "They have such a concern for those less fortunate, and it just seems that Daphne never took on that trait. You would think being raised by people so involved in good causes that she would've picked up that same character trait, wouldn't you?"

I nodded. "Both Mark and Tim are very involved in charitable causes right alongside their parents," I said thoughtfully. I hadn't really thought about this until Agatha brought it up, but it was true. Daphne never volunteered to help her parents with their charitable causes. Over the years I'd seen them get involved with a lot of different things. Usually one or both of their sons were alongside them working, but I couldn't remember seeing Daphne help out.

"Poor thing. We shouldn't speak evil of her," Agatha said after a moment.

I nodded. "That's exactly right. Daphne was still a young woman trying to find her way in the world, and I'm sure had she lived longer she would have found her place. I'll let you get back to your lunch; I've got to get cleaning up around here. It was good talking to you."

"It's always good talking to you, Rainey," Agatha said and cut into her lamb chop.

I headed over to an empty table and began clearing it of the dirty dishes. I knew the answer had to be somewhere close. Whoever had killed Daphne had to have had what they thought was a good reason to do it, and I was certain the killer would give themselves away.

As I went about my business cleaning the diner and clearing dirty dishes, my mind went over everything we knew about the case. Business had been slow today, and I hoped we'd get out of the diner early. I wanted to get home and start working on the floors in my house. Cade had been true to his word and had been stopping by after work, using the sander to smooth out my floors, but there was so much to be done in the house before the holidays.

After we had cleaned the diner and the customers had left, I buttoned up my coat and headed out toward my car. The wind was blowing, and the dead leaves from the trees were swirling around the parking lot. Sam would have to hire someone to remove the leaves once the trees had dropped all of them. My car was parked up against the edge of the parking lot, and tall trees were planted along the perimeter of that side of the parking lot. The leaves were a beautiful orange and gold with a backdrop of green grass growing along the outer perimeter. The idea of being a photographer made me happy, and I stopped and pulled my phone from my pocket. I began taking pictures of the piles of leaves, feeling a bit silly, but also kind of happy. I got a great shot of the swirling leaves that I thought would look wonderful on film. As I looked at the photo, I wondered what it would look like in a sepia-tone print. And that was when what Agatha had said hit me. Photography chemicals.

Chapter Twenty-Three

I DROVE OVER TO THE lodge, hoping to speak to Mark. He had some explaining to do as far as I was concerned.

I knocked on the door and when Lana opened it, she smiled. "Hello, Rainey," she said. "What brings you by this afternoon?"

I smiled back at her. "I was looking for Mark. Is he at home?"

"He's around back in his studio," she said. "Would you like me to call him?"

"Studio?" I asked, puzzled.

She nodded. "Yes, Mark has caught the photography bug. There's a little shed back there that he's turned into his studio and darkroom." She laughed. "You should see him. He loves nothing more than to spend hours in that shed. And I have to admit, he's gotten quite talented at what he does."

I nodded.

"I had no idea. What does he take photos of?"

"He loves to take pictures of nature. He's got his garden back there, and of course there's a great big forest and the river. You should ask him to show you some of his work. He also has some beautiful shots of Daphne," she said, and sadness crept into her eyes when she mentioned her daughter. "They're really quite lovely. Ask him to show them to you."

I nodded. "I'll do that. I'll ask him to show them to me."

"You can just go on around back, you'll see it. It's a little shed that's painted red with white trim. He insisted Bryan put up the shed for his studio. Just knock on the door and he'll let you in."

I nodded. "Thanks, Lana," I said and headed back down the porch steps. Mark was a photographer. Jack was a photographer. Had Mark started taking photos before he worked for Jack? And why had he worked for Jack for such a short period of time? Something didn't add up. Or did it?

I walked quickly toward the little red shed behind the house, my boots making a crunching noise as I walked through the dead leaves. The lodge and campgrounds would provide a lot of interesting backdrops for photographs. I wondered if Mark planned on taking photos commercially. If he had any talent, he could make decent money selling his photos.

Planted along the front of the shed were beautiful purple flowers. I had never seen anything like them, I stopped and admired them for a moment. Then I knocked loudly on the door. The shed wasn't very large, and I wondered how a dark room would fit into it.

After a moment the door swung open, and Mark stood there, looking wide-eyed at me.

"Hi, Mark, your mom said you would be back here," I said brightly.

He quickly recovered from his surprise and smiled. "Hi, Rainey," he said. "What brings you to my little piece of the world?"

I shrugged, "Your mom mentioned that you took photographs, and I am going to be in need of an updated author photo for my new cookbook early next year. The one I have now is pretty outdated. It's at least five years old."

He grinned. "That sounds awesome. I'd love to help you out with that. Would you like to come in?"

I nodded and followed him inside the shed. He closed the door behind us, and I looked around. Just as Lana had said, there were several photos of Daphne on the wall. They looked as professional as any Jack had at his shop. The photos were in color, black and white, and sepia-tone.

"Wow, did you take all these of Daphne?"

He nodded proudly. "Yes, my mother insisted I take them. I really wasn't interested at first since what I really like is taking pictures of nature, but now that Daphne's gone, I'm glad I did. I've been practicing for quite a while."

I nodded. "They're beautiful. Are they taken with film or digital?"

"Film. I find it far more interesting than taking digital photos," he said. He seemed bashful talking about his photos. It was almost endearing.

"That's interesting. How did you learn to develop the film?"

He cleared his throat, his eyes on the photo of Daphne. "Jack Farrell gave me a crash course in film developing last year. I hung out around his place for a couple of months, and he showed me everything he knew. I have to say, it's a lot of fun. Developing film, I mean."

"I bet it is," I said. My eyes went to his hand, and I noticed a faint scar on the back of his hand. "Tell me, Mark, have you heard anything new from the police regarding Daphne's death?"

He looked at me surprised. "Why are you asking me? Why aren't you asking your boyfriend?"

His tone suddenly became hard, and he seemed tense. "I don't know. It's not like Cade tells me everything. He can't. Some things have to be kept confidential. But I thought maybe the police had talked to you or your parents about what they knew, or what they were working on."

"I really don't think I believe that." He stared at me now, his eyes going hard.

I narrowed my eyes at him. Two could play this game. "What do you mean you don't believe that?"

"Everyone knows you've been all over town sticking your nose into our business. I told my mom that you are a very suspicious character and not to trust you, but she won't listen to me. She seems to think that you're a friend of the family, but I know better."

I was surprised at Mark's sudden change in demeanor. "I don't know what you're talking about, Mark. I am a friend of your family. It's true I've been asking around, but it's simply to help put Daphne's killer behind bars. That's what you want, isn't it? Don't you want Daphne's killer behind bars, Mark?"

He studied me for a moment. "Sure. That's what we all want." He moved over behind a table that he had near the back wall and began fiddling with some boxes.

I folded my arms across my chest. "What's going on, Mark? You know more about Daphne's death than you're letting on, don't you?"

He glanced up at me, but then kept doing whatever it was he was doing with those boxes.

When he didn't answer me, I moved closer to the table that was standing there. "Why aren't you answering me, Mark?"

"You know, Rainey, you're just an incredibly nosy person," he said without looking at me.

"Sometimes you've got to be nosy to get to the truth," I pointed out.

Mark suddenly leaped from his position near the table, knocking me on my back. I tried to scream, but the air rushed out of my lungs before I could get it out. His hands went around my throat, and he began choking me. "Daphne had it coming. She was a spoiled brat who got everything she ever wanted. She got my job, she got my parent's affection and everything that belonged to me. But I can tell you one thing: she isn't going to get my freedom and neither are you."

I tried to pry his fingers from my throat, but he was stronger than I was. I began gasping for air and struggling with all my might to get him off of me. It had been over a month since I had been to the gym to work out, and I realized what a terrible mistake that was.

"Don't think I'm taking pleasure in this, Rainey," he grunted while squeezing my throat. "But I don't have a choice. I'm not going to prison."

The room began to spin and my ears rang. I felt myself grow weaker, and I wished for Cade.

I clawed at his fingers on my throat, and I could hear him grunting as he fought back against my struggles. As things began to go black, I heard the door of the shed open. There was a gasp.

"Mark! What are you doing?"

Chapter Twenty-Four

I SAT ON THE FRONT steps of the Richardses' home, a blanket wrapped around me and a cup of cocoa in my hands that someone had given to me. I watched as the ambulance pulled away, empty of a patient. They had been called and had examined me, but I refused medical help. I knew I would be fine thanks to Lana bursting in and saving my life. I sat, numbly trying to make sense of things.

The beautiful purple flowering plants outside the shed were wolfsbane, containing a deadly toxin that had taken Daphne's life.

Cade was inside the house with Lana questioning her. Mark had already been taken away in a squad car. My heart went out to Lana and Bryan once again. Losing two children so close together would be devastating, particularly because one had taken the other's life. I shivered as a breeze blew across my body and I pulled the blanket tighter, taking a sip of my now-cold cocoa.

The front door of the house opened quietly, and Cade walked out and sat down beside me. "Are you okay?"

I nodded. "I'm fine," I squeaked.

"I wish you would have gone to the hospital and let them examine you there."

"There's nothing they could have done for me besides give me some aspirin and send me home," I said hoarsely and turned to look at him. "How is Lana?"

"She's about as good as she can be now that she's been given the news that her son killed her daughter. And for having caught him trying to kill you."

I looked away, shaking my head. "Terrible," I squeaked.

"It is a pretty terrible thing," he agreed. "I'm just glad you're okay. I wish you wouldn't get yourself into trouble."

"I didn't. I just came by to see how the family was doing and see if anybody could give me any additional information. I didn't accuse anyone of anything if that's what you're thinking," I whispered. My neck hurt where Mark had strangled me, and my vocal cords were bruised, making speaking difficult.

"I didn't say you accused anyone," he said mildly. "But you know I can't stand when you end up in harm's way."

"I'm not crazy about it myself," I said.

He wrapped his arms around me and gave me a squeeze, kissing me on the top of the head. "I'm just glad you're okay."

"What did he say?"

"Only that he hated his sister. She had gotten everything he ever wanted, and he'd had enough. He dried and pulverized the Wolfsbane into a powder and put it into the cider that you made. But we knew that, didn't we? The cider covered up the taste of the poison. He said he added just a little cyanide to be certain that she'd die."

"Cold-blooded," I managed to say and then took a sip of my cocoa to wet down my throat. "Completely planned out and plotted."

He nodded. "It doesn't get any more planned than that. I'm just thankful that Lana burst in on him when she did."

I had begun to black out by the time Lana opened the door, but it had surprised Mark when she walked in and he loosened his grip. Maybe it embarrassed him just a bit. Mark may not have liked his sister, but he adored his mother. To have her see him killing me may have shocked him into letting me go. That was when he jumped to his feet, completely releasing me. I had managed to keep from blacking out as I rolled over, coughing and inhaling sweet oxygen.

"Heartbreaking. Poor Lana, Bryan, and Tim," I squeaked out. Speaking was going to be difficult for me for a while. And right then I wanted nothing more than to go home and bathe my throat in some hot tea and ginger and then lay down and take a nap.

He kissed the top of my head again. "I better get you home. It's getting cold out here and you need some rest. Are you sure you don't want to go to the hospital to be checked out just in case?"

I shook my head. "I want to go home."

He stood up and held his hand out to me, helping me to my feet. I was glad Cade was my boyfriend. If I had an ordinary boyfriend, something like this would have freaked them out much more than Cade was now. Not that Cade didn't mind me getting throttled, but he'd been in tough situations before and he knew how to keep his cool.

Cade wrapped his arm around me as we walked back to his car. One of these days I was going to learn to stay out of trouble. But until then, I was going to get back to the gym and get my strength back. Next time, a killer would be sorry if they tried to choke me.

The End

Sneak Peek:

R oast Turkey and a Murder
A Rainey Daye Cozy Mystery, book 7

CHAPTER ONE

"Hi Rainey, you're just the person I wanted to see. I'll just die if you don't come and help out at the community Thanksgiving Day dinner tomorrow!"

I stopped in my tracks. Tori Wells, president of the Sparrow, Idaho, business owners association stood in the middle of the British Tea and Coffee Company with her hands on her hips. Her voice rose above the din of the busy coffee shop, and her head tilted to the side, looking at me expectantly. My eyes went to my good friend, Agatha Broome, but all she did was shrug and shake her head.

"What do you mean?" I asked Tori. I had just bought a pumpkin spice latte, and I was getting ready to take a big slug of it when she interrupted me. I didn't have any plans to help out at the community dinner. I had a Thanksgiving dinner of my own to put on for my family and a few close friends.

She chuckled, her surprisingly deep voice resonating through the shop. "Didn't your mother tell you? My goodness, what am I going to do about that woman? I asked her weeks ago to get with you and see if you would help out Thanksgiving morning. We start at 4:00 a.m. Can you make it?"

I hated being put on the spot, but I also hated turning down helping out a good cause. The annual Thanksgiving community dinner was something a lot of families in Sparrow depended on. The meal was for anyone that needed a good meal and didn't have anywhere else to go, regardless of financial need.

"4:00 a.m. is awful early," I said lightly. I had been obsessed with going over what to make for the meal I was going to cook for my own family. This year my boyfriend, Detective Cade Starkey, would be joining us, and I could hardly wait to wow him with my holiday cooking skills. I had already planned on getting up at six o'clock in the morning to get things started for our dinner, and now Tori wanted me to be at the community center at four? I sighed.

"We've got to get those turkeys roasting so they'll be done by the time we start serving at eleven," she said, moving closer to me. "I tell you, I've been working on this dinner for the past two months. I don't know what this community would do without all the hard work I put into it." She chuckled loudly. "But it's a sacrifice that I'm more than willing to make. Giving the way I do makes life worthwhile. I enjoy helping the less fortunate though. As a matter of fact, I live for it. I've got a servant's heart. I just wish others had one, too." She looked at me pointedly when she said it.

I nodded slowly, and my eyes went to Agatha again. I really didn't want to commit to this, and I felt like a heel for that. "I tell you what, I can spare a few hours in the morning, but that's really all the time I have. I wish I had known about this sooner so I could have planned accordingly." I cringed inwardly as I agreed to help. I already had so much to do that day.

"Well, that's your mother for you," she said and laughed again. "Like I said, I've been on her for weeks to talk to you about it. But thankfully, I've already got things rolling in the right direction. We just need your expertise to get those turkeys in the oven. Do you have a special recipe? We're going to use those nifty oven bags to get them done quickly, but what about seasonings? I guess I could do it myself, but I thought you might like an opportunity to help out. I think everyone should help out with community functions. Don't you?"

Tori spoke so fast I had a hard time keeping up. "Yes, of course," I said. And I did feel that way. I just didn't like this being sprung on me at the last minute. I had been carefully planning the day's meal and the time by which each dish needed to be done in order to make it to the table on time. It would be a squeeze, but I could manage this. I was almost sure of it.

She nodded. "I tell you what Rainey, you don't know how much this means to me. I've been working so hard on this, but I told you that, didn't I?" She laughed. "Without me getting things rolling, I don't know what this town would do. All these poor indigent people that have no place else to go. No food and no money. I just can't imagine being in their shoes, can you? But thankfully, we'll get this done. I've been rounding up all the business owners for donations of time, money, and food, and I have to say, things are coming together. Thank goodness I'm a planner!"

I nodded, pasting a smile on my face. "I'm sure it takes a lot of planning to bring this event together."

She nodded and took a sip from the cup in her hand. "Did I tell you my daughters are coming home from college? They're just like me. They're such givers. I know they get it from me. All I do is work, work, work, and they're the same way."

I nodded and slowly inched my way toward an empty table. The pumpkin spice latte in my hand was cooling off, and I wanted to enjoy it before that happened. Tori would keep me talking all morning if I didn't at least try to make an escape. "Well goodness, it's a good thing the community has you, isn't it?"

"Well, I can't take all the credit," she said, placing one hand on her chest and doing her best to look modest. "Lots of people contribute. And I'm so glad of that. I can't imagine what this meal would be without everyone contributing. But I'll have you know, I spoke to the mayor not three days ago, and he told me exactly how important I was to this town. I was so embarrassed. He went on and on. But I guess somebody's got to do it and no one else volunteered."

I nodded again, trying to appear engaged in the conversation. I smiled at her and turned to Agatha. "Can I get a pumpkin spice scone, please Agatha?"

"Yes and I'll serve that up with a bit of humble pie shall I?" Agatha said from behind the counter. I ignored the comment and turned back to smile at Tori. Agatha and Tori had never gotten along.

Tori turned and glared at Agatha. "Well, I don't want to keep you, Rainey," Tori said, turning back to me. "But I do appreciate you helping out. We have thirty turkeys just waiting to be stuck into the oven."

"Thirty turkeys? Where on earth are those going to be cooked?" I was stunned. I had never cooked that many turkeys at once.

"At the community center kitchen. They have ovens large enough to cook at least ten of them, plus I have a number of electric roasting pans that we'll be using. Don't you worry about a thing, everything will work out just fine."

Tori was in her late forties with short blond hair and blue eyes. She was striking at six feet tall. She liked to brag that she had been a former model, and I believed it. I could imagine her gracing fashion magazines at some point in her life.

"That sounds great, then," I said, pulling a chair out from the table. "I'll see you at 4:00 a.m."

"And what about you, Agatha? I guess I'll be seeing you at 4:00 a.m. as well, right? You don't want to let down the people of our community, do you?" she said, turning to look at Agatha. There was a smug smile on her face when she said it, as if daring Agatha to decline.

"Oh, I suppose so," Agatha said without looking at her. She came around from the front counter, bringing me a scone. "No charge, dear. You're one of my favorite customers."

"That's sweet of you, Agatha," I said. "Aren't you excited about tomorrow?" I couldn't resist teasing her. Her disdain of Tori Wells was common knowledge to most people in town.

"I can hardly wait for dinner at your house. I know everything you make will be wonderful. Are you sure you don't want me to bring anything?" she asked, still ignoring Tori.

"Well then," Tori said hesitantly. "I guess I'll be going."

I looked over my shoulder and nodded. "Okay then, Tori, I'll see you bright and early Thursday morning."

When Tori had left, Agatha rolled her eyes. "That woman!"

"Now, now, Agatha," I teased. "She's doing a wonderful thing for the community. You need to appreciate her more."

"And if I don't appreciate her, you can bet she's going to make me miserable, one way or another."

I chuckled. "You certainly aren't going to be able to overlook anything she does for the community, are you?"

She shook her head. "There's no chance of that. She'll make sure everyone knows," she said and went back behind the counter and picked up a cup of tea. "Let's have a sit and catch up."

She headed back to my table and pulled out a chair. "My mom didn't say anything to me about the community dinner. I guess I should have known better than to think Tori wasn't going to ask me to participate. It's just that time got away from me and I sort of forgot about it. I can hardly believe tomorrow is Thanksgiving."

She nodded. "I don't mind helping out at the dinner, it really is a good cause. It's terrible that so many people either don't have the money to fix their own dinner or have no place to go. It's just Tori. Let's just say she's more than I can stand most of the time."

I nodded. "I understand completely. Tori is so full of herself at times, but I try to ignore her when she starts bragging."

"I've tried that, but she gets up in my face when I do that. I told her I wasn't going to be able to make it to the community meal because I had something important to do, but she's done nothing but try to make me feel guilty ever since."

I looked at her. "What did you have that you needed to do?"

"Sleep in!" She sat back in her chair and laughed.

I shook my head. "We'd all like to do that, wouldn't we? Don't worry. It will be fun. You just wait and see. Besides, you can come in with me at 4:00 a.m., and we'll do our time together. As soon as we get those turkeys into the roasting pans, we'll be able to go home."

"I hope so. But knowing Tori, she's going to try to strong-arm us into staying the whole day," she said and took a sip of her tea.

"Oh no, that's not going to happen. I've got our dinner to put on. I've got to leave no later than 8:00 a.m."

I did enjoy helping out at the community meal, but like Agatha, Tori could get on my nerves. Every time I saw her she spent more time talking about herself that she did anything else and it quickly wore on a person's nerves. It was probably why my mother hadn't told me Tori had asked for me to come and help out. My mother couldn't tolerate people who admired themselves as much as Tori did.

Buy Roast Turkey and a Murder at Amazon:

https://www.amazon.com/gp/product/B07MMJMMRG

If you'd like updates on the newest books I'm writing, follow me on Amazon and Facebook:

https://www.facebook.com/Kathleen-Suzette-Kate-Bell-authors-759206390932120/

https://www.amazon.com/Kathleen-Suzette/e/B07B7D2S4W/ref=dp_byline_cont_pop_ebooks_1

Made in United States
Orlando, FL
22 April 2024

46083456R00107